THI
(
& OTHER DECAI

EDGAR SALTUS (1855-1921) was a novelist and short story writer whose fiction explored the decadence and cruelty lying behind the opulence of the American Gilded Age. His urbane, epigrammatic style earned him the admiration of major *fin d'siècle* figures, including Oscar Wilde and Edward Heron-Allen. His major works were *Mr. Incoul's Misadventure* (1887), a novel credited with introducing the philosophy of Arthur Schopenhauer to American audiences, and *Imperial Purple* (1892), a history of the Roman Emperors in prose poetry. He alswo wrote numerous *conte cruels* for magazines and newspapers.

DANIEL CORRICK is an editor and literary historian with a specialist interest in nineteenth-century literature, especially the evolution of Gothicism and the Decadent movement. He has worked on a number of volumes including the collected fiction of Montague Summers, and unpublished works of Edgar Saltus and Edward Heron-Allen. In addition, he has edited several anthologies, including *Sorcery and Sanctity: A Homage to Arthur Machen* (Hieroglyphic Press, 2013), and *Drowning in Beauty: The Neo-Decadent Anthology* (Snuggly Books, 2018). He can be reached at: https://dccorick.com

SNUGGLY BOOKS

EDGAR SALTUS

THE PRINCESS OF THE SUN

&

OTHER DECADENT STORIES

EDITED AND WITH AN
INTRODUCTION BY
DANIEL CORRICK

THIS IS A SNUGGLY BOOK

ISBN: 978-1-64525-099-9

CONTENTS

INTRODUCTION

DESPITE Oscar Wilde's quip about it having
gone through barbarism to decadence without
anything in between, America is not often thought of
as having made any serious contribution to Decadent
literature. The admittedly modest crop of its children
connected with that movement are eclipsed by even
the mildest of their European counter-parts. It may
be that we find it hard to reconcile some of the core
ideas of decadence i.e. cultural decay and refined
sensibilities cultivated to the point of obsession, with
the self-affirmatory independence and optimism of
the American Dream. Yet many famous names of the
movement would themselves point out that the nation
had provided an original and skilful figure in the form
of the writer Edgar Saltus. In a style both languid and
recondite Saltus wrote essays on the subjects of per-
fumes and poisonings; histories covering the infamies
of emperors and the evolution of gods; novels recount-
ing the cruelty of millionaires and the secret lusts of
heiresses. More than anything he wrote of the milieu
in which he lived, the period of national growth and
social opulence historians would later call the Gilded

Age. It is because of this that he warrants recognition, not only as a decadent writer born in the United States, but as the originator of a quintessentially American form of decadence.

Edgar Everton Saltus was born in 1855 to a patrician New York family with roots stretching back to before the War of Independence. With his generation the pattern of military officers, merchants and captains of industry that typified the family fortunes was finally broken. His elder brother, Francis Saltus, was also a promising writer: once fêted as the American Baudelaire, he lived a tragically stereotypical *poète maudit* lifestyle, dying of an alcohol related illness at the age of thirty-nine. The young Edgar was by many accounts a shyer individual, though he reportedly developed his eye for the ladies very early on in adolescence. Following a mode of education common to those of his class he completed a preparatory course in classics at Yale, after which he travelled in Europe for several years (1873 to 1878), there completing further study at the Sorbonne and later the universities of Heidelberg and Munich. It was in these places that he encountered his formative literary and intellectual influences: in Paris, through his friendship with fellow New Yorker Stuart Merrill, he was introduced to the Parnassians and Victor Hugo; in Germany he absorbed the then fashionable philosophical pessimism of Schopenhauer.

Upon his return to America Saltus completed a degree in Law, the basis for a career which by then it was clear he had neither the inclination nor intention to practise. With the encouragement of the friends made in Paris and the ever-Bohemian Francis he gave himself to literature. It was in 1884, a year after his marriage to Helen Sturgiss, that Saltus published his first volume, a slim study of Balzac. This was followed by *The Philosophy of Disenchantment* (1885) and *The Anatomy of Negation* (1886), two philosophical treatises which brought his name to the world's attention and cemented his reputation as "an unholy genius." Needless to say this alleged wickedness brought Saltus many more dinner invitations and requests from publishers. Then came his first novel: *Mr. Incoul's Misadventure* (1887). This work, on the face of it the simple story of an affair and its tragic consequences told in the most restrained yet lapidary prose, is probably the great work of American decadence and deserves far wider recognition. This was the start of what has long been thought of as the noonday of Saltus' literary career; over the next decade he produced seven more novels, having as their themes venality, disillusionment, cruelty and sexual obsession across the aristocracy of New York. The acrimonious break-up of his marriage occasioned *Madam Sapphira* (1893), a femme fatale narrative that serves as a gender switched counterpart to *Mr. Incoul*. He achieved a second masterpiece with *Imperial Purple* (1892), a compendium of impressionistic sketches of the lives of Roman Emperors from Caesar to Heliogabalus written in the lush manner of a prose poem.

The end of the century was a difficult time for Saltus. It began with the death of his brother and the break-up of the Bohemian circles they frequented. A second marriage brought him a daughter, Elsie Saltus, but also another bitter divorce and prolonged custody battle. From the 1890s onwards economic circumstances forced him to turn his energy to journalistic writing, producing articles and short stories for society magazines. Although it gave him a new target and subject matter for polemics, namely the great institution of the Press, this mode of existence chafed at the novelist, who opined that it was responsible for his literary decline. Although he endeavoured to keep abreast of social change—the 1904 *Perfume of Eros*, for instance, has as its heroine one of the "New Woman"—in general his later novels lack the tautness and psychological impact of the '80s works. The assessment of Saltus as a writer who peaked in the early 1890s is untrue, however, since until the end of his life he produced striking short fiction, which, for reasons to be discussed later, has been hitherto overlooked.

He married for a third and final time in 1910; his new wife and long-time love interest Marie was a devotee of Helena Blavatsky and an enthusiastic writer of strange fiction in her own right. Her presence encouraged him to further explore esoteric and Eastern philosophical ideas. This metaphysical evolution gave him new themes on which to write, though he lacked the energy to develop them in the long form, with one critic describing his late novel *The Ghost Girl* (1922) as unfinished sketches for a Gothic novel. More accomplished are the histories *Historia Amoris* (1906), an episodic account of Eros across civilisations, and *Lords of the Ghostland* (1907), a study in comparative religion wherein the life-denying tone of pessimism is softened by Hindu themes. Towards the end of his life Saltus and his oeuvre enjoyed a brief resurgence in popular interest through the efforts of Carl Van Vechten, whose essays presented the older writer's work to a generation eager to discover home-grown precursors to literary Modernism. Saltus passed away at the age of sixty-five in 1921 leaving his final novel, *The Golden Flood*, still unfinished.

The neglect Saltus' work fell into stems not from one single factor but an accumulation. Literary legend has it that a budding Saltus revival was crushed by a scathing article from the critic H. L. Mencken; yet this chatty little piece contained no criticism Saltus himself hadn't already voiced more forcefully and is anyway mainly a polemic against Marie's theosophical influences on the writer. Ultimately it was changes in literary fashion which drew the veil of obscurity over his works. American literature, coming into its own with High Modernism, no longer felt the need to justify itself through parallels with Europe, indeed that it had ever done so was considered faintly embarrassing. The New Yorker's decorative, sometimes frenzied style, was not a happy match to a generation raised on Hemmingway. Even sympathetic scholars of later years are mainly familiar with Saltus through the philosophical essays. In the case of the shorter fiction much of the problem comes down to location; although he published collections during his life, much of his work is scattered throughout the many magazines for which he wrote, most of which are the last place one would look for literary decadence. His habit of retitling and rewriting the same story ideas means that the discerning reader would be forced to sift through often lower carat versions of the same piece before finding its pure exemplar. Several items with notably darker or stranger themes never saw publication and exist only as manuscripts held in university archives. This volume collects together a representative selection of his work whilst a companion, *Van Almont and Other Tales of the Gilded Age*, will present more of the glittering, sometimes macabre, society stories.

Many of Saltus' short stories fall firmly into the tradition of the *conte cruel*. Even at his lightest, in society pieces such as "The Business Man," irony is seldom absent. His characters, normally writers, society ladies and wealthy men about town, allow their obsessions to distort their perception of a superficially genteel social word (as we shall see the gulf between illusion and reality is probably the typical Saltean preoccupation). As a stylist his prose is highly decorative, scented with orchids, cigar smoke and exotic poisons, but although he employs that manoeuvre—common among the decadents—of cataloguing *objets d'art*, he typically eschews elaborate syntactical construction in favour of short, often declarative sentences. Aphorisms abound; at his most enthusiastic entire scenes are summarised in epigram. Quickly gaining a reputation as an aphorist in a period in which aphorists were common, he sought to cultivate this reputation for stylistic affectation, with one critic quipping that "style was synonymous with Saltus."

In reality, preoccupation with stylistic form stems from the influence of the older French school; of all Saltus' kinship with writers of that nation it is the Parnassians, in particular Théophile Gautier, to whom he owes the most as a prose writer. Even towards the end of his life he would continue to identify himself with that movement, praising its cool amoral perfectionism and comparing it favourably to the later Symbolists whom he accuses of substituting chaos for calm and confusion for clarity. Perhaps ironically, for all his debt to France, the writer who unquestionably serves as the great model for Saltus' short fiction is his country-man Edgar Allan Poe. In some cases this influence is obvious, for instance were it not for the Belle Époque gilding "A Drama in a Dining-Room" could be a lost piece out of *Tales of Mystery & Imagination*, but it can also be seen more generally in his treatment of paranoid and obsessive psychologies, as well as the macabre eroticism with which he surrounds his heroines. Saltus looked to Poe as a precursor to literary pessimism, but the two share a deeper tradition of mystery and melancholy which makes the New Yorker one of his few *bona fide* American heirs.

His chief subject is the extravagance and conspic-uous consumption of the Gilded Age as witnessed throughout the upper class New York society in which he moved. The setting is the birthplace of a new ar-istocracy, the old colonial families grudgingly making room for businessmen, stock-brokers and industrial magnates, all poised to found new dynasties on their newly acquired millions. This vast upsurge in wealth grants a generation of aspirant bon vivieurs confidence in the face of alleged European cultural superiority; it is boom time on Wall Street and bankers are beginning to eclipse the power of kings. Of course the happiness and well-being this increase in national prosperity represents is illusory: although they may enjoy the blessings of Mammon the sons and daughters of Gotham still nurse cruel obsessions and soul-sapping maladies of the heart. A scene in one of the stories in which a character "philosophises on the degree of decomposition that renders game most savorous" to the bored and scheming attendees of an opulent banquet is emblematic of the true state of society. Subverting the anti-American snobbery common among the decadents, Saltus also portrays European spiritual sophistication as a sham; his narrators take wry amusement in observing indigent aristocrats vying for the attention of American expatriates and their wealthy daughters, even as they strive to appear contemptuous of them. The theme of great personal affluence masking disillusionment and despair would be popularised by twentieth-century writers such as F. Scott Fitzgerald, but Saltus' vision is an important reminder that, even in the pre-War years, the American national psyche feared the hollowness of its own success.

Saltus is credited as being the first to introduce the pessimism of Arthur Schopenhauer and Eduard von Hartmann to American audiences. Whilst disinclined to embrace an ethics of renunciation, he was attracted to the age old claim that the cause of suffering is desire. Such an admission puts him at odds with a cultural identity rooted in the pursuit of happiness. Early on, he implicitly sided with Hartmann to the effect that man is happiest when subject to illusion. We interpret the world according to our desires and the inevitable disparity between appearance and reality this leads to is the cause of the disillusionment which must inevitably overcome the rational man. This outcome is evinced to grotesque effect in "The Princess of the Sun" but also more slyly, in a way well recognised by aficionados of horror fiction, in "The Plot" and "The Nameless Shame." All personal attributions of philosophical allegiance must be taken with a degree of qualification, however, for Saltus was always keen to maintain a degree of scepticism and ironic distance between himself and any set world-view. Not for him is the misanthropic wit of a Twain or the bitter sarcasm of a Bierce; the New York writer is far too urbane for such *naiveté*. Later on he professed to embrace Theosophy, that rather indeterminate mixture of Hermeticism and Tibetan Buddhism, but even this was salted with a great deal of irony and distrust towards its representatives. What attracted him was a belief in the intermeshing of the cosmological and the moral, and a sympathy for the doctrine of reincarnation. In his fiction this occasional seasoning of metaphysics provides a way of linking then contemporary social settings with symbolic and supernatural episodes, as in the aforementioned stories and in the dream visions of "The Beloved," surely the darkest piece he ever wrote.

Finally, a word must be said about the process of selection for this collection. As has been mentioned Saltus was in the habit of often rewriting and retitling stories with the best version seldom being the most accessible. In addition to this, he possessed a positive mania for certain names, employing them throughout his fiction, sometimes for reoccurring characters but most often with completely new ones. Old framing devices are re-used in radically new ways. Compiling an adequate, let alone complete, bibliography of Saltus' short writings is a Herculean task for any scholar, a reason for which we are all the more pleased to offer this selection of his fiction which represents, to use a phrase most suited to the author, the cream of the crop.

Unless otherwise noted the pieces in this collection appeared in various periodicals including *Munsey's*, *Ainslee's*, *The Smart Set*, *Cosmopolitan* and *Redbook Magazine*. "Alma Adorata" and "The Princess of the Sun" also saw publication in *Purple and Fine Women*. Wherever possible comparison has been made between various publications of the same text and occasional corrections made in the light of this.

"The Beloved" and "Loveland", both previously unpublished, were taken from individual longhand manuscripts in the collection: Edgar Saltus Papers. Yale Collection of American Literature, Beinecke Rare Book and Manuscript Library. The editor would like to thank staff at that institute, as well as Jacquelyn Marie Shannon, for their assistance.

—Daniel Corrick

THE PRINCESS OF THE SUN

&

OTHER DECADENT STORIES

THE PRINCESS OF THE SUN

"*A los piès de V.*"
From what abyss of memory I dragged the phrase, the Lord only knows, but I got it out by virtue, perhaps, of what poets and gamblers call inspiration.

The lady to whom I addressed it bowed gravely, deeply, distantly, with that swan like movement which has never been customary here and which is not now frequent abroad. It is a form of greeting that belongs to an elder day. But it is very fetching. I was properly pleased, and I would have renewed the expression of my homage yet that my host prevented. Offering the lady his arm he led her, myself in leash, to the dining room beyond.

My acquaintance with both these people dated literally from that moment. I had never set eyes on either of them before. A few days previous I had left at this house, which is in upper Fifth Avenue, a letter of introduction that had been furnished me, beneficently, by one of those charming people whose names you may read in the papers every day of your life and who form what is colloquially known as the smart set. The furnishing of the letter had come about in this fashion.

I had been furiously at work on a book of the kind which when published is handsomely bound and never read. The subject had, however, absorbed me. It concerned the Incas. I knew nothing at all about them, but I had found that the best way to master a subject of which you are ignorant is to write it up.

To that end I had haunted the Astor Library. Yet in my *sćances* in those halls there were impressions, fugacious, elusive, which I just discerned and never got. To use a technical term, the atmosphere was lacking. There was not an ounce of local color in the shop. I wanted it by the pail, and there had come to me a foreboding that in search of it I might have to go to Peru.

I hated the idea of that. It is a beastly trip. Besides, at Palm Beach there was at the time a young person with whom I had interchanged all those lovely vows which mean so much and also so little. By every other post I was receiving assorted insults from that girl. It was inconceivable to her then, and has been since to me, how I could prefer the society of dead Incas to her own liveliness. And she suspected, and made no bones about saying so, either, that it was all gammon, that the Astor Library was a blind, that I was engaged on something unfathomably nefarious, and that if I did not drop it and come at once I need not come at all, *et voilà*, *etcetera* and so forth.

I was, therefore, in what I think I have seen described as a quandary. To literary people writing a book is like having a baby. Any interruption in the process is at the expense of the child. Girls never understand that. Though you be willing to give them everything you have and more, too, except one thing, your time, your time is the one and only thing that will content them. Girls are very unreasonable. This young person was extraordinarily so. It was one of her charms, and of charms she had many. So many, in fact, that I did not want to lose their possessor.

I was therefore up a tree. I knew that in sitting about at the Astor Library all the local color I could fish would find a large and ample playground on the head of a pin. I knew, too, that if I presumed to go to Peru nothing earthly would convince that girl that I was not an out and out criminal. Meanwhile there was the baby, or, rather, the book, and what was I to do?

At this juncture Providence so ordained that I took tea with the Le Grand Waldrons, who, as you know, are society folk of the toppest notch. These people poured balm all over me. More for conversation than comfort I explained my difficulties and immediately they had a cure.

"I tell you what I will do," said Waldron. "I will introduce you to Don Ruis Ixar."

"You will not have time, dear," Mrs. Waldron interrupted. "We leave for Aiken tomorrow."

"Well, I will give you a note to him, then," Waldron continued. And he did, explaining while he was writing it that Don Ruis was a Peruvian, very eccentric, very rich, very artistic, the very man to tell me everything.

"Particularly about that woman," Mrs. Waldron had interjected.

"What woman?" I had asked.

"Nobody knows. She was at the opera with him last night. The whole house was staring at her. She is a most extraordinary-looking creature."

"She is devilish good looking," Waldron corrected. "Here," he presently resumed, "is the note."

It was as a result of this note that a few evenings later I found myself going into dinner behind the lady at whose feet, through some prodigy of memory, I had been able to precipitate myself.

When, a moment before, I had entered the drawing-room, she was seated at a piano. At once Don Ruis had come to me, welcoming me in French, then he had turned to this lady, taken her by the hand and, addressing her in Spanish, had presented me to her.

As he did so I realized at once that in all my life never had I seen, or dreamed of seeing, a human being so exquisite. She displayed in their perfection the three great feminine *desiderata*—perfect figure, perfect features, perfect grace. Her eyes were pools of purple, her hair was a garland of flame, her mouth a scarlet thread.

By comparison the young person at Palm Beach, whom I had regarded as a pocket Psyche, would have, had I thought of her, looked rather plain. But I did not think of her. On the contrary, mentally I was submerged by this woman's beauty, which, from beneath the chandelier under which she stood, radiated with a light so unique that I was in doubt how to define it. It seemed to me to belong to a type of civilization more effective than our own. Mentally, as I have said, I was submerged, but optically I was dazzled. About her were suggestions of the celestial and with them evocations of the damned.

I throw that in not because I think it sounds well, but because I felt that she was a realized ideal. Yet, though I felt that way I could not very well tell her so. In the first

22

place, my knowledge of Spanish is limited to six lessons which I received in boyhood from a German, and in the second place I am slavishly conventional.

"*A los piès de V.*" (at the feet of your grace), was all I managed to get out, and how I did that the Lord, as I have said, only knows. Then she had bowed, gravely, deeply, distantly, but with ineffable charm, and on the arm of Don Ruis had proceeded, I following, in to dinner.

The table was a pleasure to look at. The cloth was gold. The plate was gold. For centerpiece there was a gold tree, in the golden branches of which there were apples of gold, the golden fruit of the Hesperides. The lusters were gold, and in dishes of gold were golden flowers.

It was all quite agreeable. So, too, was the dinner. At the latter, which a squad of lackeys served, there presided the high gastronomic muse of Savarin and of Brisse. There was, for instance, a strawberry soup the like of which I have never eaten out of Petersburg, and rarely there. For roast, too, there was a delight. Instead of the inevitable canvasback there appeared a royal cygnet, the neck arched, the feathers replaced, an orchid in its beautiful beak. For sweets, apart from this lady, who was gowned deliciously and, I assume, extravagantly, though I cannot be sure, for I lack the huckster's eye— apart from her there was but a single dish, zambalione, of which the constituents are plovers' eggs beaten with champagne into an ethereal foam.

During the progress of these and other courses equally classic Don Ruis held forth very amiably and delightfully on the subject of nothing at all.

Mephistopheles is supposed to be slim. Fancy him fat and you can see Don Ruis. His eyes were chocolate, and in them was that gleam that comes from secret and intense satisfaction. He wore a mustache and a great beard cut fan shape. Both were black, blue black, specked with gray. When he laughed, as he often did, he threw his head back, the mouth open, and in the latter I saw that his teeth, after a curious South American custom, were filled with diamonds—with little diamonds, of course. On the thumb of his right hand he wore a big one.

With that hand now and then, during the progress of the dinner and the interludes of his talk, he took hold of the wrist of the lady and, bending forward, addressed her caressingly in his caressing tongue.

On such occasions she would turn to him gravely, leisurely, with that grace with which she had bowed to me, and answer him briefly with the "*Sí*" which is "Yes" in Spanish.

Don Ruis ate largely. The lady let dish after dish go by. Infrequently she raised a glass to her mouth and touched her lips to it. Over the soup I had addressed to her in French some observation. Before she could reply Don Ruis answered in her stead, and from the subject passed to others, holding forth, as I have noted, very agreeably.

When the zambalione had come and gone I addressed her again.

"Do you not speak Spanish?" Don Ruis interrupted.

"Alas!" I exclaimed, looking not at him, but at her. "Alas! all I know is a bit from one of your singers:

Por una mirada un mundo! Por una son risa un cielo!
Y por un beso! Yo no se que te diera por un beso!

which being interpreted means: 'For a look, a world. For a smile, a heaven. And for a kiss! I do not really know what I could give you for a kiss.'"

The recitation was not in accord with my usual slavish conventionality. But something, the wine with which the squad of lackeys kept refilling my glass, the woman herself, the vistas which she evoked, all these things, perhaps others, too, must have affected me. Yet barely had the words slipped out before I was conscious of their stupidity.

I was about to say as much, to protest rather, that in letting this thing go I had done so as a beast of a parrot might; but immediately Don Ruis, bending forward again, grasped the houri by the wrist.

At that, quite as though my bad taste were another homage, she bowed to me, while he, throwing himself back in his chair, laughed longly as he bawled out "Bravo!"

Thus encouraged, I might have fumbled in memory for more stuff of the same kind, but the lady was rising. On the arm of my host she passed to portiéres which lackeys held open.

There he bowed to her, the portiéres fell, he returned to the table, where we both resumed our seats, and where presently I succeeded in extracting from him whiffs of the atmosphere for which I had come.

Don Ruis talked with a profusion of gestures, volubly, picturesquely, but so abundantly that under the douche of words my interest, already distracted, waned

25

a bit and my thoughts veered from Peru to the supernal loveliness of that woman.

Who could she be? I wondered. Manifestly she was not his wife, otherwise he would not have taken her in to dinner. Manifestly, too, she could not be a relative. He was black as hate, and she was fair as hope, fairer even, so fair that it pleased me to think that she might be an Inca, some ultimate descendant of the Princes of the Sun that ruled Peru with blinding splendor before the *conquistadors* chanced that way.

Into the core of that fancy perplexity came. I began to conjecture where and how I could manage to see her again, and I determined to cultivate Don Ruis, to be insatiable of color and atmosphere, to haunt him and his house on the chance of a word with her.

"Ah, but," he was saying, "I mind me now I have pictures of Cuzco—Cuzco, you know, the Sacred City of the Sun. I have pictures of the *coraquienques*, the sacred peacocks. Yes, I mind me I have pictures of all of these. Your permission. I will fetch them."

Rising from the table, Don Ruis passed through a door that led, not into the drawing-room from which he had come, but into some other part of the house.

As he disappeared I turned and looked at the portiéres behind which the beauty had vanished. Long since the servants had gone. The room was very quiet. But from afar I could hear the voice of Don Ruis. He was singing an air from some opera, one of Verdi's, I thought, but which? Then suddenly from behind the portiéres came a noise, slight yet noticeable, a noise much like to that of a chair overturned.

From beyond there filtered the voice of Don Ruis: "*La donna è mobile.*"

It was "Rigoletto," I told myself, that he was singing, and telling myself, too, that I might perhaps enjoy a moment with the other donna, I got from my seat, and, brushing the portieres aside, passed into the adjoining room.

There I looked in vain for the gorgeous Princess of the Sun. The room apparently was empty. Toward the further end of it the projection of a grand piano, at which she had sat when I first entered, masked a corner, and, thinking that perhaps she might be there, I went forward.

To my unutterable surprise, there immediately I beheld her on the floor, flat on her back, the skirt of her dress disordered, an overturned music stool beside her.

It was, of course, at once obvious that she had fainted. Instantly I was looking down at her exquisite face, from which, to my astonishment, her purple eyes stared up.

"Can she be dead?" I cried.

But no, that I saw was impossible. The scarlet of her mouth was as vivid as before. In her face and the lobes of her ears the pink flush of health and life was present. Yet still her eyes stared up at me.

In my heightening bewilderment I bent down.

"Madame!" I called. Then tentatively I took her hand. It was cold and rigid, very hard, with a hardness that no hand has ever had, and as with a shudder and a strangled shriek I dropped it. I divined rather than detected that this Thing on the floor was not human.

27

At the moment my brain seemed to tip. To steady myself I turned and clutched at the piano, and as I turned Don Ruis, singing still, erupted.

To have saved my life I could not have spoken, but at that Thing I pointed.

"Eh? What?" said Don Ruis in answer to my gesture. "Eh? What?"

But at once he, too, saw, and, throwing back his head, the diamonds glittering in his fangs, the brute laughed long and loud. It was a laugh like to that which Swinburne has catalogued as heard in hell, far down. And still he laughed. But at what? And why? Was I mad? I asked myself. Or was he?

"Ha! ha!" he roared. "Ha! ha! ha! *Por una mirada un mundo. Por una soririsa un cielo.* Ha ha! Forgive us, dear sir. We did not mean to affright you. Our little beauty has merely run down. One moment. You shall see."

Thereat, drawing a key from his pocket, he got down on the floor, inserted the key somewhere in the waist of the Thing, gave it a twist, another, a dozen perhaps, and stood up, raising with him that which I had taken for a houri, an Inca, a Princess of the Sun, and which I then saw was a mechanical doll.

"How delicious!" I exclaimed. Abruptly my amazement had departed.

In its place delight at such perfection of workmanship had come. "How delicious!" I repeated.

"Is it not?" Don Ruis answered appreciatively. "Is it not? And, believe me, so very agreeable to have about the house. The phonograph in her throat only says the things that I like to hear. Where is the woman who would be so particular? And no cause for jealousy, not one. But for envy! Ah! that is another guitar. At the opera, where I take her; in the park, where we drive, every man who sees her looks as though he could eat her up. And the fine ladies, they are green. Yes, green. Aren't they, Mariquita?" he added, turning to his doll.

"No, believe me," he continued, turning again to me, "with her I have peace."

As he spoke he tossed a hand in the air as though waving away unhallowed reminiscences of women in the flesh.

"No," he resumed, "she is like the rose, she charms, she does nothing but that. And so docile! A squeeze of her wrist and my way is hers. But come, Mariquita will come, too, and we will look at my pictures of Cuzco and the sacred peacocks of the Sun."

"Thank you, Don Ruis, thank you," I answered, for by this time I was tired out. "With your good leave I will come another day."

"At any time. It will be always a pleasure. Mariquita!"

Grasping the doll's wrist with one hand, with the other touching a button, he summoned a servant to see me out.

"Mariquita!" he repeated.

And as I bowed to Don Ruis, Mariquita bowed to me gravely, deeply, distantly, with the swanlike movement I had admired so much.

And I, not to be outdone in courtesy, repeated, as I backed to the door, my initial salute:

"*A los piès de V.*"

A BUSINESS MAN

IN the ornate and brilliant room, when the songbirds had flown, the musicians had departed and the last guest had gone, Duncan dropped into a chair, lit a cigar and looked at his daughter—a slim, low-breasted beauty.

To all New York, to all at least that counts, which numerically is not enormous, she had been hostess that night. Only Effingham had been absent. At thought of him a dizziness seized her, and as Duncan lit and looked, silently she crumpled. In that ornate and brilliant room she fell to the floor, her arms outstretched. It was as though death had touched her. She was ashen.

Duncan started. Old, cynical, astute, he loved her. Except for his millions, she was all he had. But now, before he could reach her, she turned, moaned. In a moment, assisted by him, she got to her knees, then to her feet.

"I'll send for Sturgis," he told her. A hand to her head, she shook it, moved away.

"But Kate! You have never fainted before. You must see a doctor."

She had reached the door. "No, I'll go to bed. I suppose I am tired."

But she spoke without conviction. Duncan followed her to the wide tapestry-hung hall, saw her to the lift. Then, entering the library, he took up the telephone, called for the physician, got him, asked him to come.

Barring *Poor's Manual* and the *Financial Chronicle*, the library was bookless. Yet not otherwise empty. The furniture and woodwork had come from the Grand Canal. One great chair was dogian. Before it, on a vast table was a winged figure, a Mercury, the work of Benvenuto Cellini, that bandit who had the hands of a fairy. It was not priceless, since Duncan had bought it, but it was in keeping with the rest of this house which gave on upper Fifth Avenue.

Now, it was not the Mercury that occupied him, but his daughter. Since childhood and its multitudinous ills, always he had seen her active, ardent, alert, the picture of health and beauty. And yet, two minutes since, after an evening not more tiresome than any other, she had fainted. For the moment he could but hope that she was not in for anything serious.

The year before she had come out. At once there were aspirants. Among others, Jack Scarlet, a young man abominably good-looking, but with nothing else to his credit and no credit elsewhere.

"No man can have my daughter, with my consent, unless he can support her," Duncan had told him, at which, Scarlet, after securing a berth in Wall Street, had returned to the charge. But Kate, who had laughed and danced with him, apparently wished to do nothing but that.

Meanwhile Solférino had put his modern, entirely authentic and equally non-existent principality at her feet. Hohenzolras had asked that she share with him the title of Serene Highness. Finsbury had offered the strawberry leaves.

In each instance the girl had laughed and refused. "I don't want to be duchess, I don't want to be princess," she told her father. "I want to be happy."

"That is the most selfish wish in the world," Duncan replied.

But the point of view pleased him. With his endless millions he had acquired the interior of palaces, the gems of galleries, the manuscripts of seers. Though a financier, he had taste and he had flair. But crowns and coronets he did not regard as assets, and what assets were he knew. What is more notable, everybody knew that he knew. In the old boom days a tip from him was a fortune, and so clearly that when Scarlet secured the berth in Wall Street, he got it by whispering, confidentially of course, that as Duncan's future son-in-law he would be provided and amply with just such tips.

Duncan, who knew all that was going on and a good deal that was not, learned of the trick. The effrontery of it amused him. But it hardly heightened the young man in his esteem.

Now, as he sat in the library, he pressed a button. A footman appeared.

"Dr. Sturgis will be here in a moment. When he comes, take him to Miss Duncan and say with my compliments that I would like a word with him before he goes."

"Thank you, sir."

Duncan was again alone, but his thoughts were many. He had scented that the time to buy had come. Stocks, after their long agony, might go lower. But he never tried to get in at the bottom, precisely as he never waited to unload at the top. Presently stocks would, he felt, be selling at double their present quotations and his instinct regarding them was due to a prescience that had enabled him to foresee in a harlequinade at Washington, the panic, rebound and slump that ensued. He had been a bear ever since. Now that everything was at its blackest, he saw the light.

"Dr. Sturgis, sir," the footman announced.

Duncan, without rising, nodded. "Nothing wrong upstairs, eh?"

The confessor of all New York—of all, that is, that counts—Dr. Sturgis had a pointed beard and a manner which if not ecclesiastic was at least sedate.

"Nothing abnormal," he replied.

Duncan smiled. He had hoped as much. "And what did you prescribe?"

Sturgis plucked at his beard. "There is no need for any prescription—at present."

"At present!" Duncan surprisedly repeated.

Sturgis turned. "Good night, Mr. Duncan."

The hall engulfed him. It was long and wide. Before he reached the outer door, Duncan was telephoning to Kate.

In her stead, a maid answered. Miss Duncan had gone to bed.

But though the girl had gone to bed, she had not gone to sleep. Sleep, latterly, had been long in coming. Not until morning would it take her, lull her, free her from herself, from the knowledge of that which was and of that which was to be.

At Newport, that summer, love had swum into her life. Hitherto she had but laughed and danced while awaiting the heart's desire which happiness is and which then Effingham had brought her.

Effingham was a widower with no tombstone to show. His wife, dead to him, to the world and to herself, was insane. But the fact had little weight with Kate, and prudence as much meaning as it has for children and for gods. There might have been a hundred Mrs. Effinghams. Love in swimming into her heart swept every other consideration away. Now and again in thinking of it all, she recalled a picture which she had somewhere seen. Entitled "Le Vertige," it showed men and women in a ballroom, and behind a slender screen, two others embracing. Their *vertige* had been hers—and his. Only—someday the screen must fall away.

Now, on this night, after Sturgis had appeared, questioned and gone, she saw another picture, one that had come to her just before she had fainted, the vision of a man with the face of a soldier and the eyes of a poet, that irresistible compound of the resolute and the magnetic which was Effingham's.

Then her father had telephoned. The picture faded, another surged—an engraving in a Victorian novel which represented an old man standing on a threshold and bidding a huddling girl begone!

Meanwhile, below, in the bookless library, her father sat. He too had his pictures. Kate's mother who had died long since. Kate as a child, Kate as a young girl, Kate as a débutante, Kate dismissing Scarlet, Kate renouncing coronets, Kate refusing the strawberry leaves, Kate wanting only to be happy. There were these. There were others. In particular, a Newport vista in which together stood Kate and Effingham. Now the silent collapse, the ambiguousness of Sturgis and at once with that insight which had made Duncan what he was, he knew. The front door had not closed on Sturgis before he saw it all.

Passionless as algebra, devoid of nerves, accustomed in any crisis to think and to act, he rang, gave directions, had himself lifted to his rooms, from which, the next morning, mentally armed, he descended to the library again.

Always in Wall Street before the opening, he had intended on this morning to be there earlier still. There were brokers to be summoned, orders to be given, details to be arranged. Instead of which, telephoning to his office that he might not be down that day, he sent for Kate.

When presently, languid and lovely in a honey-colored gown, she appeared, he got up, motioned to the chair in which a doge had throned, closed the door, took another seat, looked at the girl and smiled.

"How did you sleep?"

Kate, settling herself, answered absently: "Fairly well, father. And you?"

"Oh, as usual. Now I want to have a talk with you."

Kate who had been looking down, looked up. "About what, father?"

"About myself, of course. What do people ever want to talk about? But incidentally a little too about you.

Now Kate, things have not been going very well lately, have they?"

Kate flushed. "In what way do you mean?"

"I mean that when things do not go well, ignorant people always blame someone else, sensible people blame themselves and wise people blame nobody. A wise man knows that whatever happens, happens because it had to happen and because it could not happen otherwise. Do you follow me?"

Confusedly Kate sat back. "Yes—no. I mean not quite."

Duncan nodded at her. "I will put it more clearly then. We all make mistakes. You may have also made them. In that case I shall not blame you. On the contrary. The only punishment a father should inflict is forgiveness."

Kate turned uneasily. Was it possible, she wondered, that he knew—and already! "But punishment for what?" she got out.

"Well—for remaining single. Now I want you to marry and to marry Scarlet. Will you?"

Kate straightened. "Certainly not."

"It will be a bit awkward then. It will mean going abroad and for the moment I had other plans."

Kate now was crimson. She knew he knew. In miserable protest she half-raised a hand. "But——"

"Oh," he got in. "I know you don't care for Scarlet. He is a damned scoundrel. It is for that reason I selected him."

"But——"

"Precisely. He will treat you badly. You can leave him. I will get you a divorce and afterward it may be that you will meet someone with whom you can be happy and for me at least it is not selfish to want you to be that."

"But——"

"There! I understand how you feel. Leave it all to me. I am a business man. But in every business man's stock-in-trade there is, or ought to be, honesty and my honesty in regard to you will surprise Scarlet. But he is blackguard enough to thank his stars for even that opportunity of getting a quid pro quo in cash."

Kate had shrivelled. Pay a man to marry me! she tormentedly thought. But before she could protest again, nervously she started.

At the door a tap had come, low and discreet, and a footman appeared with a card on a tray which he brought to Duncan.

Duncan took the card, looked at it, looked again and from it looked at the footman.

"Where is he?"

"In the drawing-room, sir."

Duncan turned to Kate. "*Poor's Manual* is at your elbow. It is one of the most diverting books ever printed. You might occupy yourself with it until I return."

As he spoke, he got up, followed the servant, crossed the wide tapestried hall and entered the ornate, but now less brilliant room, in the center of which stood Effingham.

In similar circumstances there are fathers who would have reviled him, struck him, thrown him from the house. In places less ornate, he might have been cowhided, strangled, shot.

Duncan asked him to be seated. But the asking was accompanied by a look which was chill and pointed as a rapier.

With unswerving eyes, that look Effingham returned. "Mr. Duncan, I am sorry to trouble you. In coming here I asked for Miss Duncan. I was told she was engaged."

Duncan nodded. "Well, what of it?" For a second Effingham considered the question. Then out the answer came. "Mr. Duncan, I am here to ask your daughter——"

Instantly Duncan got it. But what he said was: "We are not in Salt Lake."

Effingham made a gesture. "Forgive me. I should have told you. Mrs. Effingham died yesterday. Though in her condition she has been dead so long that——"

On with it he rambled. Duncan had ceased to hear, ceased rather to listen. The large fact occupied him. It overshadowed Scarlet, Europe as well, besides being just the thing. Mentally he waved it. But he said and simply enough: "And you want my daughter, is that it?"

Effingham bowed. "A year's delay is usual I know, but in the circumstances——"

Duncan, hastily swallowing something, caught him up. "Am I to understand that my daughter has already encouraged you?"

It was but a sprat for a mackerel, which at once Effingham produced.

"Not at all, sir. On the contrary. Moreover I have not been in a position to expect encouragement. But I had thought that with a divorce—one which death has unexpectedly granted—I might ask."

You are a cool customer, Duncan thought. Yet the decency of it appeased him. "Well?" he threw out.

"I believe you knew my father," Effingham resumed.

But that was coals to Newcastle. Duncan had not only known him, he knew practically to a dime how much he had left.

"I am quite able to support your daughter," Effingham continued. "If——"

There shall be no ifs, Duncan decided. But he said: "There is an if in everything. My daughter has refused many offers, some perhaps more advantageous than yours. But I do not believe in interference."

"I have your consent then?"

Duncan stood up, took out his watch, looked at it, put it back and looked at Effingham.

"You will find my daughter in the library. But I have to go. It is after the opening and I am a business man."

LOVELAND

IN Paris, on a carnival night, in a dining-room that was fitted with plenty of taste and some of it even good, a manservant slept. Before him was a table on which supper had been set. Behind him was a stand on which stood a telephone. Violently the latter rang. The servant stirred, started, went to the stand and in a voice that was soft as mayonnaise addressed the instrument

"Yes, madame. Pardon, madame, I was in the kitchen. Yes, madame. The Bulgarian caviare, the Belgrade duck, the Montenegro salad, the Cubist sweets—all the fashionable dishes."

Respectfully he paused then added "Perfectly, madame." At once, bowing to the telephone, he put the receiver up, reseated himself and yawned.

The minutes limped. Suddenly another bell sounded. The servant vanished and returned, ushering his mistress, Diane des Baisers, an actress famous for her beauty, famous also for other things less beatific.

The lady was in a honey coloured gown and a salmon hued cloak. She looked sumptuous and soulless. Behind her trailed four men in evening dress.

Of these men, three were typical *viveurs*—reprobates is perhaps a better term. But the fourth obviously was of another world. He was stalwart and sombre with dense blue black hair and brilliant eyes.

From over a shoulder Diane cried, "A moment, my little dears," and paced into an adjoining room.

One of the reprobates, a little man with a monocle and a carefully ironed moustache, surveyed the table and exclaimed, "Red duck, green salad, yellow pastry, eh! Rather rainbow."

"What I like," said another who contrived to look both young and old, "is a foam of pheasants and the maxims of Sardanapalus."

But the third, who was bald, drawing the others aside and indicating the fourth man said lowly: "Who is that chap? He looks like——"

The little man, dropping his monocle, whispered, "Diane picked him up at the ball."

"Or he picked her up," the admirer of Sardanapalus suggested.

The little man patted his moustache. "Suppose we introduce ourselves." In speaking he turned, moved over to the stranger and affably addressed him. "Sir, my business is pleasure and I am called the Duc de Vannes."

Orientally folding his arms the stranger gravely bowed. "Inexpressibly charmed."

Meanwhile the others had approached. "Sir," said the Sardanapalian suavely, "my name is Guy de Ruy." With a gesture at his companion he added: "Let me make you acquainted with my friend and brother-in-Loveland, the Comte de Caracole."

With the modesty of the well-bred, the count described himself. "My occupation is dressing and undressing."

"And digressing," the duke with a laugh threw out

"I," said the stranger, "I am nobody and——"

"But that is an immense advantage" de Ruy cut in, "Won't you be seated?"

"That is to say," the stranger resumed, "I know nobody and——"

"But that is an even greater advantage," the count interrupted, "won't you take two seats."

"No, take the table," cried de Ruy.

"But not the supper," laughed the duke.

"And my business is danger," the stranger managed to announce.

Understandingly the count nodded. "Then we are all in the same trade."

"Yes," de Ruy caressed his chin, "Yes, for woman is danger."

"And here," laughed the Duke with a bow to Diane who at the moment was sweeping stunningly in, "here is Danger in its most delectable form."

Vivaciously the actress indicated the table. "To supper, my little dears."

But de Ruy was attempting a step. "The tango first."

Caracole, attempting another, exclaimed: "A bit of a hug."

Laughing, the duke stretched his arms. "A big one!"

Diane laughed too. "No, supper first and then——"

"Permit me," said the duke, who from the table had taken a goblet which he raised. "During the supper the Deluge and after it——"

"Shut up," the actress told him seating herself as she spoke at the head of table. "And you," she continued to the Count, "sit next time. And you, Guy de Ruy, there. And you, duke, there. And you," she added to the stranger, "there—where I can look at you." She turned to the servant, "Sylvain, the wine!"

Under the cover of a popping bottle, Caracole, after a glance at the stranger, whispered: "Who's your friend?"

Prettily, with the air of an ingénue, Diane whispered back, "A man whom I do not know."

"He rather looks like Sandor, don't you think?"

"Sandor?" Diane, as though vaguely perplexed, repeated.

Caracole, stuffing himself with caviare, nodded. "Yes, Sandor, that Brazilian who killed himself because of you."

In the most natural way, Diane gave a little shrug. "I have forgotten."

"It is only a month or so ago," Caracole between bites, retorted.

Indifferently Diane smiled. "A month or so is a life-time."

"Or a death-time," the stranger gravely remarked.

Diane gave a little start. One might have thought a pin had pricked her. "What?" She exclaimed.

The stranger bowed. "It must be such a luxury to lay one's life at your feet."

"Eh?" said Diane. Then she giggled. "For a million-aire you are very gallant."

Under cover of more popping, Caracole whispered: "Is he a millionaire?"

With a peek at her plate Diane nodded: "So I hear"

Caracole, emptying his glass, nodded also. "So was Sandor."

Diane showed her teeth and uneffectedly the vixen snapped at him: "To the Devil with you and your Sandor."

"Beautiful one," the duke, half rising and craning, called at her. "What an odd ornament you have on your fourth finger."

"You think so," the lady, negligently removing and exhibiting a ring, replied. "My nurse gave it to me."

The duke reseated himself. "Your nurse? A very dry one then. If it did not sound rude I would wager it's paste."

"Put it up at auction," Guy de Ruy suggested. "Yes, and a kiss or two with it."

"What am I bid?" the lady, entering into the sport of it and instantly assuming the role of Venus Auctioneer, exclaimed.

Caracole raised his glass. "A handful of gold pieces."

"Two of them," cried de Ruy.

"Four—and on all fours at that," laughed the duke.

"And you?" Diane asked the stranger.

For a moment, without enthusiasm, he considered her. Then in level tones he called:—"My heart."

Diane tossed the ring at him. "It's yours."

"Ah, very good," said the duke. He was rising. In marked disgust he addressed his friends. "We are out of it. Let's go to my aunt's."

"Your aunt's!" de Ruy with every appearance of alarm exploded. "Why there?"

"It will be gayer."

"And the supper not finished," Caraocle protested.

The duke looked him over. "Never finish anything, that's the true philosophy of life and love."

Indicating the telephone, he turned to Diane. "You permit?" Without waiting for her consent, he went to the instrument, and, after the usual discreteness, the customary delays, asked of it: "Is that you, Aunt Clotilde? How is your dance progressing? Ah, I see, not enough men. May I come and bring reinforcements? What? I did not quite hear. Oh, where am I? I am closeted with the archbishop. Yes, yes. He sends his blessing. Very good, in ten minutes."

Abandoning the telephone, he turned again, nodded at the stranger, gestured at his friends, who abody had risen, and saluted Diane. "Beautiful one, au revoir."

"Au revoir!" de Ruy chorused.

"Au revoir!" chimed Caracole

"Au revoir!" Diane flung at their retreating backs. "Au revoir indeed," she resumed. "They must be all very rich." She turned to the servant. "Au revoir to you."

Meanwhile the stranger had also risen. Now as the servant departed he moved over and seated himself beside Diane.

"A bit old fashioned, your guests, eh?" he now asked.

"Perhaps," the lady languorously answered. "But I rather specialise in bric-a-brac."

Cavalierly the man considered her. "And am I to be added to the collection which I may assume is rather vast?"

"Well," she murmured, assuming as she did so a look of candour which was intended to be infinite.

"What if a woman has been kissed, her mouth does not lose its freshness for that—or for you."

With entire unconcern the stranger lighted a cigarette. "You see," he presently told her, "I am an epicure."

"Yes?" she prettily put in. "Now just what is an epicure?"

The stranger inhaled the smoke and exhaled an aphorism. "A man who finds peculiar charm in postponing the fullest pleasure." He paused and added, "I have one in reserve."

Diane, framing her mouth into the sketch of a kiss, smiled at him. "Is that it?"

For answer the stranger but looked at her. And what a look.

But Diane had got it now or thought she had. "Ah, ah, ah!" she lulled. "You mean my heart. But because you have given me yours it does not follow that I shall give you mine."

Then she paused and bewitchingly lisped. "And yet I may. Do you know when I first saw you I thought you were——"

"Somebody else?"

"The handsomest man in the world."

Darkly the stranger nodded. "But not in the grave."

"What?" she surprisingly exclaimed. "What do you mean?"

The stranger gestured. "I have come from—far over there—to tell you."

But now again she had got it or thought she had and again she laughed. "You had heard of me? No, you had seen my picture! My picture, well, sometimes it is in the papers. Only yesterday——"

"Yesterday has gone," the stranger interrupted. Dropping his cigarette into Caracole's empty glass he added, "And tomorrow has not come."

At the obviousness of it she clapped her hands. "The present is ours."

The stranger sniffed. "That plural is singular."

"The present is yours then," she seductively corrected herself, "if—if——"

"If what?"

But though the lady hesitated it was only that she might employ all her arts. "Tell me," she resumed, "at the ball tonight somebody pointed you out and said, 'There's an American millionaire.' Then I smiled at you. Oh, believe me, not on that account at all, but because you are so handsome and you—you remember?—you came up and spoke to me."

"Eh bien, après?"

"But it is true is it not?"

"Is what true?"

"That you are a millionaire?"

"I am not a pauper."

In contentment of it Diane sighed and smiled. "There! When a man says that, he is always rich. When he says he is rich, go take a walk, he is a crook."

"Probably," the stranger with complete indifference threw out.

Diane giggled at him. "Oh, I know. Over there you saw my picture and you came to find the original. Have not I guessed right?"

"I certainly came to find you,"

Diane beamed. "And now that you have, what are you going to do?"

The stranger stood up. "I'll tell you later."

"Always the epicure," Diane, rising also and trying to be funny, exclaimed.

At that, for the first time the stranger smiled. "Yes," he muttered, "and sometimes the executioner?"

"The what?" asked Diane who had not heard, for in speaking he had moved from her.

"A term we use over there," he replied and stopped and looked her up and down. "You may not know about my country. It is a land of passion loves and passion hates. Yes, and passion fruits."

"Oh," cried Diane. "How glorious!"

Grimly the man assented. "Yes and when the fruit gets here it is sucked dry and thrown away."

Savorously she stuck out the point of her tongue, "How I would like the same!"

Significantly he nodded. "You had me"

"I?" Diane in real surprise, exclaimed.

"Straight from Brazil."

She started back. "From where?"

"From Brazil. Did you not hear me? I said Brazil." The words came from between his teeth in a whispered hiss. But to her there must have been then the blare of twenty trumpets. A moment before she had started. Now she shook. It was as though something were shrivelling her. It was as though too he had dropped a mask. Her beauty, where was it? She was ghastly.

"I am Sandor," he was telling her. "Sandor, brother of the man you first ruined then deserted."

But now palsy had got her. She shook. Yet the actress was in her still. She tried to smile. The grimace of it contracted her mouth and she stammered.

"W—w—why, w—w—what do you m—m—mean?"

Calmly Sandor told her. "I'll show you." But however calmly he spoke, there was that in his eyes that withered.

In the blight of them panic seized her. "No, no. Listen. I—I——"

She might as well have addressed the dead. Sandor caught her, pinioned her, dragged her to the adjoining room.

"Help! Sylvain!"

The door closed on that cry. From behind it another filtered. At once Sandor, smoothing his tie, pulling at a cuff, reappeared.

As he did so, through the other door, the servant entered.

"Did you call, sir?" the latter, in his mayonnaise voice, inquired.

Sandor nodded; he was lighting a cigarette. "My hat and coat. Then get me a cab."

For a second he inhaled the smoke. Immediately with a gesture of finality, he tossed the match aside.

THE PLOT

"HAS the *Figaro* come yet?"

It was at Nice, in the reading room of a cosmopolitan club. A little before, I had dined on dishes that a poet had prepared. Now, for after course, and although I had a novel under my arm, I wanted to look at a paper.

"Pardon, monsieur," said the servant to whom I had spoken. "Behold a gentleman who is reading it."

I had beheld the gentleman before. That morning I had seen him on the Promenade des Anglais, and that afternoon I had seen him again in this club, where I had heard him talking over the green baize at baccarat. He was a pleasant-looking chap in Saville Row clothes, which he wore with a sort of studied negligence. He wore also a monocle, and his voice was deeply Belgravian.

In that voice he addressed me: "You are asking for the *Figaro*. Let me relinquish it to you."

As he spoke, he got up from a chair in which he had been seated, and approached me, the paper in his hand.

In my own hand was the novel, a story by Eric Hereward, which I put on the table before us.

He glanced at the book. "Do you find it interesting?"

"I have not opened it," I answered. Before he could say more—that is, if he had intended to—Spencer Poole, an Englishman whom I had long known, sauntered up and joined us.

"If this is a private conversation," he threw out, "I should like to hear it. Otherwise, I will go away."

"You may," I told him. "We were talking opiates."

"Let us all go," Poole affably resumed. "There are a thousand louis in the bank. Don't you want some of them? I know I do."

"I would rather not add to them," I remarked.

But already Poole had turned, the other man with him, and I followed them into an adjoining room, where, about a long, oval table that was colored with bank notes, with hillocks of gold, with patches of cards, a crowd of members were gaming.

The room, saturated with tobacco smoke, resounded with brief exclamations, with the announcement of points. Fronting it, two windows that reached to the floor opened on a balcony and the night.

Idly, after a moment, I passed through one of them. A chair stretched its arms to me. Above were the stars, and beyond, on the inky sirup of the Mediterranean, a warship rode. The vessel was strung with lights, and from it, faintly over the waters, a tinkle of music came.

"You don't play?"

I turned. The man who had offered me the *Figaro* was drawing a chair beside me.

"You see," I said, "it seems to me that there is but one thing stupider than winning money you have not earned, and that is losing it."

He adjusted his monocle. "What I like is the hazard of it. Yet is there such a thing as hazard? I hardly think so."

He paused, got out a gold case, offered it, and, on my declining, extracted a cigarette, lit it, and, a bit ponderously, inquired whether I believed in fate.

"Not after dinner," I told him. Ordinarily I would have said nothing of the kind, but I divined that he wanted to use me for a sewer, and, at the moment, I did not care to be so employed. Yet, civility prompting, I added: "Why do you ask?"

"Because I fancy that anyone who really thinks—so few people do think—must believe that somewhere—beyond, above, yet about us—there is a power that knows neither mercy nor wrath, but that compels every cause, great or small, to work out its inevitable results."

"Let me," I interrupted, "translate you if I may. 'As you mete it to others, so shall it be measured unto you.'"

"Precisely. You at least believe in that?"

"Whether I have dined or not, I do."

"I am glad to hear you say so. I have such a curious case in point. Would it bore you if I run it over?"

I felt that it would, but I assured him to the contrary, and for surcease let my thoughts wander among the stars. When they returned to earth, or, more exactly, to the balcony, he was telling of a maiden's beauty:

"Fancy a lily that for perfume has a heart, and you may perhaps see Janet Mar as I saw her when, for her perdition, she came to Stratton. In my life I have seen nothing fairer. Her hair was a turban of gold, her eyes were pools of purple, her features were those of a Psyche on a fan, and she conveyed just that suggestion of immateriality that the old masters gave to figures whom they represented as floating off the canvas into space. A painter would have admired her for what she expressed, a poet would have loved her for what she was.

"That, from the ambush where it lurked, fate should have sprung and felled a human flower such as she is explicable only on a theory that I will set before you. But that the point of it may be clearer, other pictures must be shown, and primarily that of her brother, who was her twin, and who worshiped her as only a twin brother could worship a sister so adorably constructed, and so constructed to be adored.

"Together they completed one another. What was fragile in her he made up in strength; what was material in him, her spirituality attenuated. Had you not known they were brother and sister you would have said: 'There is the ideal couple!' In some former life perhaps they were."

"What!" I exclaimed.

"Well, yes, why not?" my companion rejoined. "For if we believe in fate, it is difficult not to believe that we have been here before. Nothing else explains the inequitable inequalities of life. Nothing else explains why some are rich and some are poor; why some are wise and many are not; why some are strong and others weak. Nothing else can give the reason of our joys and sorrows. As in former days, we have meted it to others, so now is it measured unto us.

"Yet, of course, the theory is, I admit, heretical, and if I offer it, it is because it is the one hypothesis that frames this girl. Without it, she would present but a fair portrait smeared, and wantonly smeared, with mud and with blood.

"But now, to fill the picture in, a detail is necessary. When Janet and her brother Hubert came to Stratton, which, as you may know, is a village in Surrey, they were in mourning for their father, who but recently had left them, and who had left them, moreover, with means so slender that Janet gave lessons and Hubert wrote.

"If there are two more beggarly ways of making a living, I have yet to hear of them. Tennyson, I believe, got a guinea a word. For five minutes' instruction De Reszke, I understand, gets as much. But there has been but one Tennyson—though there are two De Reszkes. For the horde of other teachers and other writers, rates fall sheerly from relative munificence to absolute minims. Sometimes they lack even that.

"Sometimes Janet and Hubert supped on dry bread. Sometimes they had cheese with it. But they knew— what epicures rarely do know—that Epicurus never had more and Cæsar frequently less. They were poor, but they were young, and it is a form of genius to be that. Besides, they worked, and I always pity those who do not, though, of course, we both know people who pity those that do. But am I wearying you?"

The question reminded me of Doctor Johnson, who, asked by Boswell how he would feel if he were alone in a tower with a baby, replied that he could not be more vilely distressed than he was. But I am less brave than

Johnson, and I hope more polite. As a consequence, I lied. Yet obviously my companion did not expect me to do otherwise. He accepted the lie for what it was not worth, and ran on at once:

"You have now, then, not the frame—that will come in a moment—but the picture. That is, you see that while Hubert hacked in Fleet Street, Janet toiled at home; or, more exactly—and what is worse—in the homes of other people. To children who would never succeed in more than hiccoughing French, she tried to impart the proper *façon de parler*. With others, who had as much taste for music as those who detest mathematics have for algebra, she connived in the murder of Chopin. And for what? In the States a scullion would have been better paid.

"But everything happens because it has to happen. In the course of the lessons, she saw that which she mistook for the recompense. She saw the splendor of splendors, the face and flaming wings of Love."

"He is becoming lyrical," I tormentedly reflected, and felt, if possible, more Johnsonian than before. To be alone with a baby is bad, but to be alone with a bore is bitter. For relief, I tried to pretend to myself that I was not there. I even succeeded, I think, for a minute or two I lost him. When I caught up with him again he was playing another air.

"That was, I think, the case with Janet. She had never loved before, and, now that she did love, the universe became concentrated in this individual who to her was the Unique. To Hubert he was a very ordinary person, the form and substance of that curious thing that is called Antipathy. He said as much and more—and might have saved his breath, for Janet was madly in love with this man, who, at the time, was quite mad about her.

"But madmen have lucid intervals. I have told you of Janet's beauty; I have told you, too, of her poverty. The one was a charm, the other a douche. Beauty her lover wanted, but also he needed coin. To give the due to the devil, who usually takes it, I have no doubt that in the first fevers, which are so contagious, he meant well by the girl; but to certain temperaments the menace of moneyless matrimony is, perhaps, a febrifuge. Do you not agree with me? Do you not agree, rather, that circumstances alter kisses?"

"Yes," I replied. "Particularly reduced circumstances."

"Precisely, and there you have what dramatists call the central situation—a delicious girl wildly in love with a brute whom she considered an angel. The fellow had a keep of his own, and little or nothing to keep it up on—a gaunt, gloomy Tudor affair which had come down to him, and which, unless repaired, would come down on him. Around and about were secular trees that made it all the gloomier. A moment ago I mentioned Tennyson. Somewhere he tells of 'the moan of doves in immemorial elms.' That line will give you the place."

"I don't want it," I threw in.

"No, and you will want it less when I tell you more. Where was I?"

"In the central situation."

"Ah, yes. Well, now enters the other woman, the widow of an astronomer who had died of sunstroke. Her grief for his death, which, if abrupt, was not disagreeably paradoxical, could not have been excessive.

In any event, such as it may have been, it was at least assuaged by the fortune that he left her."

"And which," I hazarded, "appealed to the brute."

My companion gestured. "And which, as you say, appealed to Lord Cullen. Now, you will think, we are in the thick of it. Wait a second and you will find it gets thicker. For at the moment—that is, when the blue eyes of the widow's check book first entranced this man—Janet was unconscious that he was looking into other eyes than her own.

"Not so the widow. She was discerning possibilities in Cullen, who, instead of following the traditions of his caste, and marrying a Gayety girl, had become engaged to a governess. But, if discerning, she was decent, which, of course, the brute understood, or, rather, he realized that no decent woman, however discerning, would consider a man who was the property of another.

"The point with him, therefore, as you may see, was to fight free of Janet and then lay siege to that check book. Already mobilization had been secretly begun. Then came the call to arms, a bugle blast blown at Janet.

"Cullen told her that with him everything was going to the devil, that he could barely maintain a servant. But poverty had no terrors for this girl, who supped, when sup she did, on a crust, and she answered him with smiles.

"Now, however perverse a cad may be, he cannot beat down a dog simply because it loves him. There are limits even to human turpitude. Then, too, I have never known a man, good, bad, or indifferent, who would not prefer to brave mythical redskins, than face a woman's tears. Janet had shed no tears as yet, or, if she had, they were but tears of joy. The fanfare had been so much music to her.

"Seeing which, Cullen varied his tactics. He defiled into his keep, and from that stronghold wrote Janet a dozen pages, pages in which sordidness struggled with grammar, pages that one word would have covered, pages that said only 'Finis.' Only that! Only the trumpet's note that heralds an eternal silence."

After that fine phrase, which I had heard before, my companion stopped to light another cigarette. Then at once he was off again:

"I was not with Cullen when he committed that crime, and I cannot tell you how he felt; but I may tell you that when I heard of it I felt that there was no man living whom I envied less. Yet even now I must omit to judge him. We are all of us strangers to one another; not infrequently we are strangers to ourselves. The motives of human actions are not always for human ken. Because of the fate prepared for him, it may be that, whether Cullen wished to or not, he was impelled to act as he did."

"Yes," I told my companion. I no longer felt like a boor with a baby or even with a bore; he had got me at last. "Yes, for among all our uncertainties, this perhaps alone is certain—never do useless events occur."

"Never," he repeated, "no matter how useless, in our blindness, the events may seem to us. And that fact, while it applies to Cullen applies also to Janet. I was not with her, nor, poor child, was anyone with her when she got that infamous letter; yet had all the world been with her, she still would have been alone. In the great crises of the soul, everyone is, and Janet was so thoroughly alone that she could not bear it. When at last her brother found her, she had gone."

"Gone?"

"With a hatpin she had run herself through that aching heart of hers, which, because of the ache, she well knew where to pierce."

At this, I shifted in my chair, and, whether because of the night air or the story, or both, I shivered. Through the window behind me drifted the hum of talk. From beyond, over the inky sirup, the music from the warship came.

"Beside her was Cullen's infamy, and beside that, one line: 'I forgive him, and may God forgive me.'"

"And Hubert," I asked, "was he as generous?"

"Would you have been?"

"You see," I answered, "when ignorant people are injured, they blame others; the wise blame themselves; the evolved blame no one."

"Quite so—when the injury is personal. But if it affected someone for whom you deeply cared, would you not then take reprisals? It is a case of conscience, no doubt. Yet, in any event, Hubert did, or at least attempted to. He secured a pistol, and went straight to Cullen, whom he found seated beneath one of his immemorial elms, and occupied, if you please, with a copy of *Punch*. At sight of Hubert, at sight, rather, of the menace of him, he sprang up. Point-blank, Hubert fired. Cullen dropped, and Hubert, turning the pistol, killed himself."

"Killed himself also!" I exclaimed.

"No, not also. Cullen was not touched, or but barely touched. The bullet singed the hair above an ear, and lodged itself in the elm. In the elm, mind you, not in Cullen. But the imminence of death, combined with the unlordliness of the lord, did, at the moment, for him. He fainted and toppled over. It was then that Hubert, fancying him dead, turned the pistol on himself. What do you think of it?"

"What do I think of it?" I repeated. "I think that the dice of destiny were strangely cogged. It was Cullen who should have died, Cullen only. What had Janet done that she should have been forced to kill herself? What had Hubert done to have a similar fate?"

My companion raised a hand. "How do I know what they had done? All I know is that Cullen appeared to have wronged them."

"Appeared to!" I exclaimed. "That seems a bit colorless."

My companion readjusted his monocle. "Perhaps. But not from the standpoint of anterior lives. According to the theory of it, we none of us can be injured except by those who embody our past. Whatever we suffer comes from there. People who harm us are but puppets come to claim such debts as we ourselves have incurred. Apparently Cullen was but an ordinary brute; actually he may have been the hand of fate."

"Not a very clean one, then," I had to protest. "Fate, I think, might have deodorized him."

"It did," my companion replied. "And there is the remarkable part of it. By the way, are you superstitious?"

"Oh," I answered, "when the new year begins on the thirteenth, then, like everyone else, I am apt to fear it may be unlucky. Otherwise, superstition seems to me the parody of faith. But why do you ask?"

"Because Cullen developed a curious dislike for the tree before which he had been shot at. The estate was entailed, and legally he had no right to lop so much as a branch. But he took the law in his own hands. While he was about it, he took an axe. He might as well have used a penknife. But Cullen, who had two deaths to his debit, was not to be balked by an elm. He bored a hole in it, and inserted an explosive. That explosive——"

My companion paused, leisurely lit a fresh cigarette, exhaled the smoke, considered me.

I prodded him. "Well?"

He nodded. "That explosive discharged the bullet that Hubert had fired, the bullet that had been intended for Cullen, but that, having missed him, had bided its time, there in the tree, until it could, and did get at him."

"You don't mean——"

Again my companion nodded. "I do. I do mean it. The bullet went straight through his throat, and severed the carotid artery. Lord Cullen was dead. What do you say to that? Don't you think it was fate?"

What I did think was that it seemed rather odd that I, who read the papers, had missed an account of a matter so unusual, and I was about to say as much when my companion stood up.

"I should much like to stop and talk it over with you," he obligingly resumed. "But," he added, indicating, as he spoke, the warship, "I am due on the *Thunderer*. They are having a dance there. Good night."

Feeling that I had been having something of a dance myself, I turned and watched him go.

He passed through the open window into the room from which we had come, and, as he passed, I saw him stop and say a word to Spencer Poole.

A moment later I, too, got up, and entered the room, which, as before, resounded with the call of numbers, the announcement of points.

"Who was that chap?" I asked my friend.

But Poole, his eyes on the cards, did not immediately answer. Then absently he looked at me. "What chap?"

"The man that just spoke to you, the man who was with me in the reading room when you joined us."

"Oh, that fellow? Why, I thought you knew him. That's Eric Hereward, the novelist. Has he been rehearsing one of his plots to you? If so, I can sympathize. He did it to me."

THE BELOVED

IN a sea of delight Alma floated. Above were stretches of blue wadded with pink. In the waters that lapped her were roses. The air was strong and fragrant. Blissfully she inhaled it. Then, magically, after the manner of dream, she was on a bare expanse in a great building that was filled with faces. She could hear, as it welled from her, the music of the words of the Segnetto per Esses Felice—the Secret of Happiness which she had solved and of which she was singing. Through the words and the music and the meaning of them came the crash of applause. That too, and blissfully also, she inhaled. At once, without transition, she was running affrightedly through a gray darkness. Behind, running too, hastening terribly after her, was an entity not human, a shape abominably twisted and covered with sores. But now it was on her, it had got her——

With a cry she awoke.

At the window, a wooden-faced woman was letting in the sunlight. From beyond came the drip-drip of water in the bath. Without, a vagrant was yelping an air that was both melancholy and vulgar.

Alma turned. At the vision the horror of it, perspiration had started. But now, in amusement at herself, she smiled. She was so happy! The idea of dreaming such things! The smile remained, lingered rather, then passed. Suddenly, an ache in her heart prompting, she remembered Nizram had gone.

Nizram was her lover.

A year previous, Alma Adams had come from California to Paris with an uncomfortable accruement of unbecoming clothes, a letter of credit, other letters equally creditable, but with larger assets; health, youth, beauty and a voice, and what a voice! A voice that bore with it melbas, flutes and cornets, a voice so adorable that, at the very first audition, Jambuzini—the super-excellent trainer who for a generation had launched practically all the song-birds worth launching—the Jambuzini then, fumbling as usual in her wig, had cried: "my child, your phrasing is of a vileness! But when you have learned to breathe, you will no longer be Alma Adams, you will be Alma Adorata."

The name stuck. In it she was to be billed and then begin the career of prima donna which, saving only that of royalty, is the most opulent of all.

Meanwhile the unbecoming clothes had long since been replaced by the confections of poet-modists, the girl's beauty had heightened; moreover, with work such only as the Jambuzini could exact, perfect surety of phrasing had come. Apparently Alma did not even have to heat her throat. Apparently she had but to part her lips and there! a seraph was singing.

Her success, private as yet, or at least as private as anything can be in that market place which Paris is, delighted her. But everything delighted her. Personally, I have never seen a human being who so radiated the joy of life. Yet then, admired as she was and, I think, not improperly conscious of it and also, if you please, at the threshold of glory, the joy that she radiated was but natural. In addition it was contagious. It affected people; among others, Nizram Khan.

Nizram, a Persian and an attaché d'ambassade, was a new passenger in that rather rakish craft which is known as Jont-Paris. I once heard a woman declare that he was the handsomest man in the world. Well, as for that, he was good-looking, as Muhamadans of the better class often are, but to me he was entirely antipathetic. In his eyes which were false and sleepy, there was something at once impenetrable and obvious. It was as though morally he squinted. However it may have been with others, those eyes gave me a glimpse of his soul—if he had one.

It was but little over a month prior to Alma's approaching debut that he had come from Teheran to Paris and it was at the house of an American that he met her. The meeting, to supply a localism of the land, was, for Alma, the thunderbolt. When you work hard, you sleep hard, the ego is in abeyance. Hitherto the girl had had no time for love, no thought or experience of it. But in that meeting her senses awoke, they stunned her, flushed her, tripped her tongue and this girl who sang like a seraph, stammered. The thunderbolt had felled her.

Presently it all became unutterably delightful. The world was transformed and life, from a joy, was lifted into a festival. Fancy a blind man dazzled! Hitherto, in spite of gala aspects, Alma had not seen, she had not felt, she had but groped. With the coming of Nizram, presto! The grub was a winged thing, the bud had flowered. It was then that she glowed, her beauty heightened, her eyes deepened, her voice took on a richer note. It expressed then, the one thing it had lacked, passion.

At that supreme revelation, the Jambuzini twisted her wig. Her prophecy had come true. But the fulfilment was not entirely due to this lady.

Then suddenly, in apparent agreement with the troubadour who sang that the briefest of follies make the best *amours*, Nizram was off and away.

But he was to return. He had assured Alma of that. Yet had he needed to? She judged his heart—such as it was—by her own.

One morning, a little after he had gone, Alma awoke with a cry. A shape, projected perhaps from the astral, had seized her. But the cry exorcised it. In amusement at herself she smiled. She was so happy! Shortly the Beloved would be with her once more. And then! And then!

But that day there was much to do; Alma got from her bed to the bath and presently, a peignoir about her, seated herself before a mirror. A wooden faced woman approached and brushed her hair. It was very beautiful as was all else that was Alma's. But the girl, a note book

66

in hand, was not thinking of it. She was going over the arrangements for the day which was to end with a dinner at the house of the compatriot where the Beloved had taken her by storm. At the thought of him, the book slipped from her. She recovered it, opened the drawer of a table beside her and put it in there, where other things were, though, most noticeably, a pistol which Alma had carried in the Sierras that are surer than Paris.

At the sight of the weapon, the wooden-faced woman tightened her lips. But in recovering the book, the girl's peignoir had opened. It disclosed her neck, the ivory of a breast. Just above the latter was a redness. Alma, the drawer closed, leaned back, looked in the mirror and saw it.

She turned to the woman, "Why! what can that be?"

The woman, lowering her head, peered and pronounced.

"Mademoiselle has perhaps been eating mussels or perhaps mushrooms. Great gods! what they call mushrooms! But mademoiselle need not distress herself. It will pass."

"Yes, but you see, tonight I am dining out."

"A little powder then. Truly——"

But Alma got up, went to another room. The day with its roulades and appointments had begun. Later, an application of *blanc liquide* masked the irruption. Yet on the morrow there it was, redder, larger, uglier than before.

Again the wood-faced peered and pronounced. "If mademoiselle were a monsieur I would say the barbers itch. My man had it. It is nothing. I'll run to the apothecary. A little salve and good-day."

But Alma stayed her. Only recently the Compatriot, at whose unforgettable house she had met the Beloved, had dreamed that a spider bit her in the face. It may be that a spider did bite her. Anyway, when she awoke there was a red mark on her cheek as big as a silver dollar, and she had rushed off and consulted a dermatologist, Dr. Bel—Del—Mel, yes, that was it, Dr. Melmont, whose office was in the Rue Cambon, and who had given her something which at once removed it. And Alma decided that after morning exercises she too would consult him.

But the roulades did not go very well that day. The room in which she practised held but a piano, a stool, two chairs and a table. There were no hangings, no rugs. It was all rather a sounding board and on this morning, from the adjoining bedroom, she could hear the woman moving about. The fact annoyed her and it amazed her that she should be annoyed. But at once she was conscious not only of irritability but of a sense of malaise, that feeling of being aware of your bones and aware too of something irksome about them. It could not be, she reflected, that she, who had never known illness, was going to be ill and now, of all, times; on the eve of her debut and the Beloved's return! It was not possible. She would not be ill. She determined she would not and the determination, as is frequently the case, seemed helpful.

None the less at noon she was in the Rue Cambon where she sent in her card and where presently Dr. Melmont received her.

Bravely, in the direct American fashion, Alma went straight to the point, described her symptoms and bared her breast.

Alma began at the readjustment of her dress. When she had finished, Dr. Melmont still held the card but he held it absently as though thinking of some other matter.

"Well, Doctor?" Alma tentatively threw out.

With an uplift of the chin, he turned. "You are the Miss Adams whom Madame Jambuzini——"

Girlishly Alma laughed and nodded. It gratified her that she should be known to this stranger.

Abandoning the card, the physician added: "Then, if reports are true, you have been some time in Paris"

Again Alma laughed and nodded.

"But not in the East?" Dr. Melmont resumed.

"In the East!" Alma repeated. In California, the East might be Kansas or even Iowa. "Why yes," she exclaimed. "I came here by way of New York."

"I meant China—or thereabouts."

But now Alma understood less than before. The fact was patent to the physician. Again he looked at the card.

"Miss Adams, could you make it convenient to be at home at three?"

"Certainly, but——" Actually it was the reverse of convenient. At three she had an important essayage. She was about to say as much when he caught her up.

"At three then I will come with a colleague."

"But Doctor," Alma protested, "it is not serious, is it?"

The physician lowered his eyes. "Reassure yourself, it may be nothing."

As she spoke, he touched a button, and accompanied her to the door where a footman showed her to her motor.

As she entered the car she wondered what on earth he had meant with his China and his thereabouts. But promptly she forgot it. There were so many other things more important and, to begin with, the essayage. Meanwhile she was due at Jambuzini's. On her way there she stopped at the modistes, found to her relief that they could just as well have her at two. Then, after a final canter at the trainers, she returned to the dressmakers and, the fitting properly effected, reached home just before the arrival of the physicians whom she received in the music-room.

Melmont presented his colleague and in a moment, when Alma had again bared her breast, the latter examined her.

A Viennese and a specialist, he was grave, tall and, save for one curl, quite bald.

As he bent over the girl the sight of the topknot amused her. She did not smile but her eyes danced. Life still was a festival. But abruptly he raised his head, shot a glance at Melmont, turned away.

Melmont approached her. "Miss Adams, while you are arranging your dress——" A gesture completed the sentence.

But Alma understood, she smiled, passed from the room, closed the door and instead of arranging her dress was about to change it when, from the adjoining room, a dialogue filtered.

"She has some skunk to thank for that."

"I was right then?"

"Absolutely. It is the Asiatic variety, the most malignant of all."

Alma cocked an ear. What in the world were they talking about? But the dress claimed her. In attending to it, she thought what tedious people physicians are. All she wanted was a prescription. Vainly she wished they would give it and go. Again anew the dialogue came:

"Yes, the hospital and the sooner the better."

"But what a pity, a girl like that! If you could have seen her today when she to my office! She was pleased as a child just because I knew who she was."

At that, Alma turned. Was it possible that they could be taking of her?

"Oddly enough," the Viennese was saying, "recently I had a similar case. But in this instance it was a man. You know about it, though."

A pause followed, a chair creaked. Then Melmont took it up.

"Girls ought to be taught. But I see that they are teaching them in Germany and in the States too. Sex hygiene——"

"Yes, yes," the Viennese interrupted. "I agree with you entirely. But shall we ring? She has money one may suppose, Herr?"

Yet even as he spoke, the door opened. At the threshold Alma stood. She had gone quite white and she was twisting her hands.

"Forgive me, I overheard, I did not mean to. But tell me, tell me this, it is all I want to know. It is not of me you were speaking?"

Uncertainly the two men looked at each other.

"But it can't be. Why don't you say so? This person is someone who is to go to a hospital. That cannot be me. I am not ill. You can see that I am not. And I am to have my debut and I am expecting—I am expecting a friend. But why don't you answer me."

Gravely the Viennese intervened. "Mademoiselle, believe me, you shall be told whatever is necessary. But beforehand, will you tell us please where are your parents?"

Tormentedly Alma considered the man. The question frightened her. What had her parents to do with it? "In California," she blurted.

"You have no relatives in this country?"

"None."

"And this friend whom you are expecting?"

Alma flushed. She was still twisting her hands. "But—why do you ask? Do I have to tell you? But you don't know him. He is a Persian. Yes. Oh! Why do you look at me like that?"

The Viennese half raised a hand. "Mademoiselle, be assured, were you my own daughter, I could not wish to treat you with greater consideration. But without précising, without too unprofessional conduct, yet for your guidance I may say that among the local faculty it is a matter of common knowledge and therefore not a secret that in a Paris hospital there is now an attaché d'embassade who is suffering—well from a malady which, commonly, is only clinically mentionable but which he contracted in Teheran and may have transmitted here."

He hesitated, then paused. Something in Alma's face answered him. He had intended to hint merely. He had been too clear.

Like a flame, the truth burned into the girl. The fear of it withered her, her brain tipped, she reeled. Into the chaos of her mind leaped the memory of the dream of the saurian that had pursued her, felled her, blighted her. And that was the Beloved! The corrosion of it shook her. Her hands had ceased to twist. They had gone to her head. With eyes that saw but nameless shapes, she started. Then, struggling with spasms she turned. Behind her the door closed. In a moment, not far from where she had gone, came the crack of a pistol, the sound of a fall headlong.

THE GHOST STORY

I

IN the club's deserted library, where I was writing, I
looked at the clock. It marked two. Earlier that night
I had been to the opera with Cally, a physician whom
I had nicknamed Cagliostro—a pleasantry which he
openly resented and secretly liked. The best of us have
our weaknesses. Afterward, abandoning him, I had
stopped in at this club, where I found a note from an
editor asking if I could not give him a story with a
surprise in it.

"Well, I can try," I somewhat immodestly reflected.

Thereupon I had gone up to the library, and with the
glimmer of an idea—poor, certainly, but my own—was
just getting at it when, precisely as a character in fiction
marches in on you, Bradish appeared.

It was a little while, though, before I stopped. Then
I looked up.

II

Bradish was one of the few really rich men of my acquaintance with whom I had a thought in common.

But then we had, or, more exactly, used to have, affiliated virtues. Formerly his nature had been that of a sundial. It was only serene hours of which he took count. For a literary person, that is in the order of things. For a supertaxed plutocrat—with a birth mark—it is a feat.

There were other ties. I had always known him, and I was best man at the tragedy of his wedding, which had occurred a few months before. Since then the sundial quality had faded. He had become moody and remote.

Yet, at the moment, as he marched in, it was not moody that he seemed, but excited. Straddling a chair, he gestured.

"I've seen her!"

The birthmark on his face resembled nothing so much as a big spider. Usually a dull brick, it was then bright red, and I wondered if he had been drinking.

"I saw her as I see you," he added. "Just as plainly."

"Saw whom?" I asked.

He twisted.

"Why, Nelly, of course."

Nelly had been his wife—that is, if you can so describe a girl who, five minutes after the wedding breakfast, was a corpse.

Whether or not he had been drinking, it was, I felt, only sympathetic to humor him, and I nodded.

"Yes, occasionally I see her also."

It was true. I had only to close my eyes to evoke that girl who held herself so rarely that she gave the impression of having jewels and flowers about her, and whose lips, lifted at the corners by the upturned comma of the Athenian mouth, seemed parting and meeting for love.

The scarlet spider flamed.

"I tell you, I actually saw her—saw her in flesh and blood."

"Well," I answered, "there is no such thing as mystery; there is only ignorance, and with that I am abundantly supplied."

He was civil enough to agree with me.

"But," I continued, "the long and short of it is that you have seen someone who resembles her."

"Nobody resembles her," he retorted. "In all the world there is no one like her. It was she." He paused, and gloomily added:

"I suppose you think me crazy."

I smiled at him.

"I would think you abnormal if you were not. In open court here, Spitzka, testifying as an expert, said that all men are insane. In France, Janet said the same thing. Do you object to the evidence?"

He laughed fiercely.

"Only in so far as it concerns you."

At that I laughed also. "Well, then, you see, I am in good company. But seriously now, you know as well as I do, and probably better, that alcohol or morphine may produce hallucinations which, though actually seen, represent only the observers' mental condition."

He waved at me.

"You are talking rubbish. I don't drink, and I don't take morphine." I sat back.

"Certainly not; but any strong emotion can have the same result. I don't mean to bore you, but I know it to be a fact that the attendants at morgues have to be constantly on their guard against the false identification of the dead. People go there distracted by grief at the loss of a relative, and with the image of that relative so fixed on the retina that they identify the first body they see."

He glared.

"I did not come here to exchange stupidities. My mind is as clear as a bell." Again I nodded.

"And so, you will admit, was Balzac's. Balzac intended to give Gautier a horse. He omitted to, but he talked so much about it that he believed he had given it, and used to ask Gautier how the horse was. From that you can realize what the imagination is. Now you imagine that you have seen the late Mrs. Bradish, whereas you know perfectly well that that is utterly impossible."

He stood up.

"I not only saw her, I saw her with Austen."

As he said that I was back at the wedding and behind it, in the recesses of the heart of the girl who had been in love with Austen, and who would have married him had it not been for her harridan of a mother.

Well, I thought, jealousy is an emotion more violent even than grief. Jealousy, too, can produce hallucinations. But I said:

"When was it?"

He sat down again.

"Today. They were coming out of the Splendor. I was passing, saw them, tried to take hold of her, but they got in a taxi and went off." He hesitated, and gloomily resumed:

"She never cared for me. She told me so. Oh, she was frank enough about it; but I thought that after we were married I could win her."

"You see," I lamely got in, "Austen, as we all know, had been interested in her. You remember that, but in remembering it you forget the psychological fact that a man becomes interested, not necessarily in one particular woman, but in one particular feminine type. Austen has probably met someone who resembles her. Affection is merely an instinct when it does not happen to be a habit."

I would have run on, dosing him with further platitudes, but he interrupted.

"You still think me mistaken?"

"What else would you have me think? Mrs. Bradish, who was Mrs. Bradish only during the space of the wedding breakfast and for the few minutes you were with her in the motor, is dead. I was at her funeral. It is brutal of me to insist, but——"

He looked down, then up.

"Do you know what a Dorothy ring is?"

I did not know, and I told him so.

"It is a collection of little jewelled rings set one on top of the other. They are not common, but Nelly had one which she always wore on the fourth finger of her left hand. Today, as she got into the taxi, I saw it."

"You are singularly observant," I said.

"There you are," he again interrupted. "I told you I am not here to exchange stupidities. I am here for help."

It is a great privilege to be in a position to help anyone, no matter whom, and I said as much.

"Well, then, I want you to see Austen and get at the bottom of this."

But though it is a privilege to help, it is awkward to interfere. Yet the fact that he wanted me to showed a gleam of sanity. It showed that he was not sure.

Consequently, though I did not relish the mission, I agreed.

"I'll see Austen tomorrow," I said; "or rather today. It is tomorrow now."

With that he got up, and in a moment he had gone.

III

In search of a possible explanation, I groped mentally back to the tragedy of the wedding, during which Nelly Chilton had seemed less human than divine.

Except in art and story, Proserpine never existed; but Swinburne has told us how she looked. Nelly Chilton was the ideal Proserpine. Her charm was of just that quality that transforms men into pagans and lackeys—occasionally, too, perhaps, into seers; for, while I may be in error, yet I think that that charm of hers affected even the clergyman. The "Amen" with which he concluded the ceremony trailed away, without finality, as though in uttering it he had seen some uplifted fringe of the curtain that masks the future to us all.

Then at once Mrs. Chilton flung herself at the girl. The old harridan was weeping, as presently she was to weep on the wedding-cake; but the tears were tears of joy, relaxing tears that trickled into the cosmetics on her face.

Only an hour before the girl had been in open rebellion, had vowed she would not marry Bradish. Until the ceremony was concluded, the woman had trembled. Until the "Amen" had trailed away, she could not be sure. Then she was, and she wept with thanksgiving.

She had turned the trick. Austen was dished. Crœsus was her son-in-law.

Nelly shook her off and turned to Austen, who ordinarily appeared very insolent, but who had been considering her with angry and famished eyes.

Through the mortgaged windows that overlooked the Hudson came the breath of June, the smell of lilacs, the rare radiance of the day.

The house itself, a stone structure, ugly and comfortable, had formerly, when such things were, been a manor. After the fashion of other manors, the grounds contained the family vault. In the old days when we had a landed gentry—a gentry otherwise landed since—the quick and the dead dwelt together.

Meanwhile we had all gone in to the wedding breakfast, one that had arrived from Delmonico's an hour before, and for which Bradish's account had been charged. Briefly, to the amazement of a Fifth Avenue waiter in evening dress, the clergyman said grace. That over, I stood up, toasting the happy couple; but Bradish made no response, unless an uplift of the chin and a heightened glow in the scarlet spider could be so construed. He hated anything of the kind. He hated forms, usages, conventions, and it was just for that reason that Mrs. Chilton had asked no one. For Austen, whom that girl had insisted on having, did not count, or rather counted no longer, and the rest of us, the clergyman, the bridesmaids, the waiter, and myself, were but negligible auxiliaries among whom Mrs. Chilton must have felt herself lumped.

In the circumstances it would have been a bit dreary but for the clergyman, who was in fine form and kept it going. Otherwise, even the bridesmaids—two girls who were so much fresh air, and who previously had chattered like birds—were dumb, stricken so by the attitude of Austen and Mrs. Bradish, neither of whom ate or drank or said one word.

It had been arranged that, breakfast over, Bradish and his bride were to motor in to town, and the girls and myself, together probably with Austen and the waiter, were to take a train that left a little later. But no one can command the future.

The breakfast over, off they went, in a shower of rice from the girls, and accompanied by a slipper that hit the mechanician. Then, as we learned later, the motor, speeding on, had thrown a wheel, reared, reversed, crashed over, and the girl who looked like a seraph perhaps became one.

The mechanician, too, was killed; but from the great iced bath that death is, Bradish swam up. Not at once by any means. He had a broken collar-bone, which is nothing. He had also an occipital lesion, which is the reverse.

The local physician, who examined him, shook his head. It was, I could see, very empty.

This occurred in the Chilton residence, to which Bradish and his dead bride were taken, and where the local physician ascribed Nelly's death to heart failure superinduced by shock. Subsequently Cally arrived with a squad of nurses, and Bradish was carted to his great white house in town.

Meanwhile—prior, that is, to Cally's irruption—the funeral was held in the same room in which the wedding had been solemnized, and where there were the same girls, the same clergyman, incidentally Austen, and incidentally, too, your servant. Only Bradish and the Fifth Avenue waiter were lacking; but in their place were a baker's dozen of relatives, who rather filled the room and masked Mrs. Chilton from me. I caught but one glimpse of her face, which—rouge not being mourning—was unpainted.

Through the mortgaged windows came the same breath of June, the same scent of lilacs, yet mingling then with the subtler fragrance of lilies that banked the open coffin, in which Nelly looked in death as she had in life, as though conscious of and surrounded by the ineffable. Her lips, half parted, showed the nacre of her teeth, and in their upturned comma was a smile. As death came, it may have brought some vision of the supernal.

"I am the Resurrection and the Life!"

The sonorous and exalting words stirred me. I looked up at the clergyman and from him at Austen. That insolent air, where was it? Savagely he was staring, not at the dead, but straight ahead—at nothing, or else at life, which sometimes can be as empty.

The ceremony at an end, a little man, silent but fussy, whom I had not previously noticed, superintended the coffin's removal to the hall, where it was closed. Shortly we followed it to the vault, where perhaps the shades of departed Chiltons greeted the spirit of their kinswoman who, forty-eight hours earlier, during that other ceremony, may have despairfully wished for the peace that was theirs—or, more probably and more desperately, had wished that Bradish were Austen.

On the train to town, in which were most of the other mourners, I did not see Austen; but I heard one of the girls say that he had motored himself up in a touring car. Assuming that he was motoring himself back, for I could not imagine him lingering with Mrs. Chilton, I forgot him and his hungry grief.

Ultimately, through Cagliostro's wizardry, Bradish recovered. But it is only the evolved who realize that any misfortune is a boon, and Bradish had not attained that high level. Previously the sunniest of men, he became black and bitter. That, perhaps, was part of his punishment—one that he shared, no doubt, with Nelly's mother, for always it is a perilous thing to constrain a girl against her will.

IV

In the deserted library where I sat, and where the panorama of the tragedy unrolled, suddenly I recalled something which, after the smash, Cally had said to me concerning Bradish's condition:

"Lesion of the occipital cortex."

Ignorant brute that I am, I know precious little about the pulp behind the forehead; but then I am unaware of anyone who does know much. Its mysterious processes are almost as obscure today as they were to Hippocrates. Yet, though generally I know no more than the law allows, and frequently not as much, at the time I did happen to recall that an injury to the occipital cortex may result in impairment of vision.

At once I sprang up, intoning "Eureka," conscious that I had nailed it, that I had got the clue, that Bradish's sight was affected, and that that was the obvious and rational explanation of the delusion to which he had so obstinately clung.

That explanation, I later determined, would go down all the easier if compounded with other simples; and that afternoon I went to Austen's club—a little place just off Fifth Avenue, where a fat hall-porter was civilly ignorant of everything except that Mr. Austen was not about.

"Hello!" I heard someone exclaim. "Come in, and let's have the latest gossip from Parnassus."

Before me was Brevoort, a good chap, not overburdened with intelligence—which is perhaps the characteristic of good chaps. When he had got me seated by a window in the main room, he continued:

"There is only one rule here. When a member has a guest in, he has to stick to him until he bolts. Pretty severe, eh? Now, what 'll you have?"

"A line on Austen," I told him.

"Anything with it?"

"Yes, water without any ice."

With deep melancholy he considered me.

"Except water with ice, there's nothing else." He turned to a servant. "Some Apollinaris. Now," he resumed, turning to me, "I'd like a line on Austen myself. I saw him yesterday with well, I never saw anything finer. Know who she is?"

I let it go.

"Bradish says she is his wife."

"Austen's?"

"No, Bradish's—Nelly Chilton that was."

Blankly he stared. Then abruptly his face lightened.

"By George, now you mention it, I'll be shot if she did not look like her!"

He paused, indicated the water which had been brought, filled a glass, and inquiringly threw out:

"You don't believe in ghosts, do you?"

"No, but I am dreadfully afraid of them."

Yet as I uttered that antique and stupid jest, I realized that what I did fear was Bradish, whose error, I saw, was not due to any impairment of vision. What he had seen, Brevoort had also, and I startled myself by thinking that what both had seen might in truth be a ghost.

But, as I afterward recognized, that idea was due to contagion. Spiritism, psychism, occultism, abnormal phenomena—these things were in the air and quite as infectious as the flu. Only recently I had heard a more or less unauthenticated story of a young woman who had fallen so dead in love with the ghost of a youth that she eloped with him; but that, I decided, was ridiculous. Deciding, too, that a ghostly Nelly was equally absurd, I was about to say as much to Brevoort when, warningly, he raised a finger.

"Sh! There he is."

Through the wide entrance came Austen. Tall, slender, insolently good-looking, he stopped at the center table, nodded at us, and took up a paper.

With a gesture at Brevoort, I got up and approached him.

"How do do, Austen? I saw Bradish last night, and——"

He threw the paper down.

"Tell him to go to the devil!"

"Certainly not," I answered. "I'll carry no such message."

He raised a hand to his mouth, and, as though to press something back, for a second held it there. Then it fell, and he said civilly enough:

"Yesterday Bradish attempted to take hold of—er—ah—Miss Fellowes, who is a guest of my mother. You will oblige me if you will advise him not to presume to do so again. His behavior was outrageous."

"Good day," I said, and turned on my heel.

As I did so, he must have turned on his, for when I again reached Brevoort he had gone.

"You seemed to be having it hot and heavy," Brevoort pleasantly suggested.

"Well, anyway, I have laid that ghost. It appears that she is a Miss Fellowes."

"Fellowes! Fellowes!" Brevoort surprisedly repeated. "Why, that's it, then! Miss Chilton's mother was a Fellowes. The fairy Austen was with must be a cousin, and that accounts for the resemblance. Have a cigar?"

"No, thank you," I answered. "I'm off."

V

And I went. In a taxi, a few minutes later, I was driving past Cally's office, and the next minute I alighted at Bradish's house, which, big enough for a regiment, did not happen to contain him then.

"Mr. Bradish is motoring," one of his many servants informed me; "but he left word, if you came, would you please wait. Yes, sir."

The room into which he then showed me was furnished gravely, with infinite taste. I had always liked it. With a view to my comfort, no doubt, the man returned with offers of refreshment, returned again to switch on the lights, returned once more with the evening papers. Then, at last, Bradish himself appeared.

He was in a cap and a long coat, hideously beggoggled, and, as I afterward realized, he must have been curiously and even desperately calm.

At once I gave it to him about Miss Fellowes and Brevoort's cousinly deduction. With a smile, I added:

"Austen says you are to keep off the grass."

Without visible annoyance he nodded, removed the monstrosities, threw them aside, and remarked quite casually:

"Brevoort is an ass." For a moment he looked down and away and then at me. "Mrs. Chilton never had a brother or even a sister. Nelly has taken her mother's name—that is the long and short of it."

I was about to protest, but he waved at me.

"I have been there, been to the Chilton place, been in the vault. Nelly's coffin is open and empty."

When he appeared, I had got up; but at that I sat down, mentally thanking Providence that Cally was neighborly, mentally, too, trying to evolve some theory that might pacify him in this new hallucination.

"Empty," he repeated. "And there is nothing emptier than an empty coffin."

He is as mad as a hatter, I thought; but I said:

"See here, I am no good at this sort of thing. Suppose we have Cally in. Perhaps he can tell us the time of day."

He had turned from me, but he turned back.

"Very good, I'll send in and ask him over to dinner. Meanwhile, if you don't mind, I will just get some of the dirt off of me."

I nodded at him as he went, and told myself that he was cracked. On his wedding day he had been nearly done for. On recovering, he had been told that his bride was dead. He had not been present at the funeral. He had not seen the girl, as I had, in her coffin. Yet all these circumstances must, I decided, have contributed to this idea of his—an idea fixed and erroneous, which is insanity's surest proof. It is an enormous pity, I reflected, and I wondered whether he would have to be put under restraint; for obviously he could not go around pulling young women about.

These futile meditations were interrupted by the entrance of Cally, who, with eyebrows that were a bit upturned, a beak of a nose, a pointed beard, and his usual air of intense satisfaction, looked absolutely Mephistophelian.

I fastened on him at once, telling him as quickly as I could what had occurred, outlining the symptoms, and deducing from them my diagnosis—at which, very rudely, he laughed.

"Pure poetry," he told me. Airily he dismissed the subject. "What are you writing now?"

"Checks," I was about to reply, when Bradish came in.

He gave Cally a hand and, indicating me with the other, said:

"I suppose our friend has been giving you the gist of it; but he has got it wrong. There is a conspiracy against me. I did see Mrs. Bradish. Moreover, as I personally ascertained today, her coffin is empty."

Cally, who had held on to him, peered into his eyes, lifting the lids as he did so. Then, releasing him, he straddled a chair.

"Well?" Bradish asked. "Am I crazy?"

Cally smiled his Mephistophelian blandest.

"Not more so than anyone else. You may have a delusion or two. What of it? Delusions are very serviceable to people who do not have to work for a living. They help to pass the time. Yours, however, are not very complex. You say that there is a conspiracy against you. When a man can't get what he wants, he always says that. It is a perfectly normal statement. As for your other remarks, they only show that you are a bit out of touch. From recent experiences of my own I am inclined to think that unburied young women, are all the fashion now."

At the door a man appeared and mumbled. At that, we all went into the dining-room, which, while not unreasonably sumptuous, was satisfactorily sedate.

"The last time I was here," Cally put in, when he was seated, "you gave me something fit—a pheasant cooked with oranges and almonds in Madeira and tea—which of course is the only way that it could be cooked. But what were we talking about? Oh, yes, the fashion in ghosts. Though I must say that venison flavored with vanilla and served on a sofa of quinces is not a dish to which I object. No, thank you," he added to the man who was attempting to provide him with champagne.

"You won't drink?" Bradish inquired.

"Why should I? I feel perfectly well. It is idle for me to attempt to feel better."

With an eye to the dramatic, I prodded him.

"What about those ghosts?" Cally, finishing with *caviare tsarkief*, nodded.

"Not long ago I was called in consultation. The practitioner who had preceded me—a most excellent man, thoroughly reliable in benign cases of coryza—had mistaken the patient's condition, and had certified accordingly. He saw death where I found suspended animation." He turned to Bradish. "I have always maintained that the best test of death is decomposition. In the case of this patient, decomposition would have supervened had it not been for human intervention. That's my story."

"It is a bit sketchy," I said.

Cally, after an interlude with his fork, put it down.

"Now, how greedy you are for details! Well, here are one or two. Did I say that that excellent practitioner saw to it that the patient had a funeral? I did not? Then I will now. But in the neighborhood there happened to be someone so infatuated with the dear departed that for a spectral *tête-a-tête*, a ghoulish kiss, a Stygian farewell, or perhaps just the mortuary memory of a sepulchral vigil—something, anything, which, unseen, unshared, he could take and keep and cherish forever as his very own—that monster—hey, a bit of bread!"

"Go on, hang you!" Bradish angrily threw at him.

But Cally took a little roll, broke it, nibbled, and with exasperating blandness asked:—

90

"Where was I?"

"In the middle of Poe's complete works," I serviceably put in.

"Oh, yes! Well, that demon—but look here, did it ever occur to either of you that respectability can be singularly corrupt? Take a cheesemonger, or—or take an auctioneer—don't they exude respectability? And yet in their hearts what abysses there may be!"

"The champagne you did not drink has not gone to your head, has it?" I engagingly inquired.

Cally, ignoring me, nibbled anew, and pushed his plate back.

"I tell you," he ran on, "you never can tell. I have in mind an undertaker whom I suspect of being a church-warden, and what could be more respectable? And yet I know him to be a villain. Yes, sir! That devil of a chap—from the middle of Poe's complete works— bribed the sanctimonious villain to dilly-dally, to wait a bit, to leave the lid of the coffin temporarily ajar—and with what sinister purpose you are aware. Then, undercover of night, he went to the tomb, removed the partially open lid, and, divining rather than recognizing what my predecessor, that excellent practitioner, should have known, he carried the dear departed to a car, hurried with her to his home, and sent for me. Dear me, it was just a case of suspended animation. I had the young woman on her feet in no time. No, that is an exaggeration, for she had a broken ankle; but yesterday I saw her lunching at the Splendor. As I said, unburied young women are all the fashion today."

"Damn your fashions!" Bradish shot out. "Was she with Austen?"

Cally resumed his fork.

"I could not say. I did not notice. But it was a Mrs. Austen who called me in. Nice old woman, but—er—what is it now?"

Bradish, the spider on his face flaming as it had never flamed before, and almost, I could have sworn, extending its scarlet antennae, flung his napkin on the table, overturned his chair, and, before the mutely startled servants, hurried from the room.

I started to follow. With a gesture, Cally stayed me.

"Let him be. For the moment he is better alone."

"But confound it, Cally, that was Mrs. Bradish you were telling about, and I, the Lord forgive me, thought——"

"What is this?" he asked of a man who was presenting a dish. Then he turned. "No, not Mrs. Bradish. Mrs. Bradish is dead—legally, at any rate. The certificate of her death is entered and filed."

"But——"

He half lifted a hand.

"From now on she can call herself what she likes. She can even decide to be known as Mrs. Austen, as, some day, she probably will."

Well, later, she was so known, but not until a Western divorce had facilitated her second nuptials, at which Bradish vehemently refused to assist. It was very small of him. I told him so, told him that the gallant rescue deserved applause; but, very nonsensically, he had got it in his head that it was all a put-up job. Steadily, carefully, he cursed Austen and was about to revile the bride—who had been his bride, yes, and the bride, too, of death—when abruptly he stopped, and in the sudden flash of silence I saw that, perhaps, for the first time, he realized how evil it is to constrain a girl against her will.

VI

In the deserted library where I was writing, I looked at the clock. It marked two.

Then I read it over.

That ought to do, I immodestly reflected, and, signing it, I stuffed the manuscript in an envelope, directed it to the editor, yawned, and went home.

DRAMA IN A DINING ROOM

IN the multiple brilliancies of the dining-room I found myself at the left of the Duchess Sally. Ever since her girlhood I had known her. At Narragansett Pier, in the good old nights before the Casino was dreamed of, I had sat with her on verandas that were vibrant with osculations. That was some time ago. Her subsequent transatlantic triumphs and spectacular marriage to the Duc de Malakoff are now ancient and familiar history—so ancient even that I am dispensed from noting that Sally is no chicken. But though her youth has gone her heart is young. Hence, no doubt, in disregard of every canon of precedence, my place beside her. But then, as I have intimated, she never was ceremonious.

Across the glittering service, beyond the gold branches of the lustres, sat Monsieur de Malakoff. Between him and Sally there were, including myself, fourteen other people. Over the bisque I had taken them in. Barring a nuncio and an aunt of Sally—Mrs. Nicholas Manhattan—I knew none of them. Barring two others, the rest of the party interested me but mediocrally. Of these two one was a vision in white, a delicious apparition that suggested the *pays des songes*, a face infinitely delicate and of exceeding beauty. The other was a young man who looked as the musketeer Aramis might in modern dress. His features were chiseled. On his lip was a mustache that seemingly had been drawn with a crayon. His hair was black, slightly curled; his eyes were chocolate, and their lashes long as a girl's. I should have thought him too good-looking for a man had it not been for his chin, which was resolute, and the expression of his mouth, which was as firm and as chill as steel. Next to him was the vision. They were talking inaudibly together.

The bisque had gone. The *maître d'hôtel*, followed by *valets de pied*, was presenting sturgeon from the Volga. Turning to Sally I asked who the young man was.

"The Marquis de Parabole," she answered. "That is his wife, next to you." Sally would have said more, perhaps, but the nuncio was claiming her attention.

Already I had noticed my neighbor, a little, red-headed woman, who, in face and manner, suggested a bird—yet, perhaps, a bird of prey. In any event, a bird that, with beak and talons, knows how to defend its own. In the word or two that I had already exchanged with her I knew by her accent that she could not be French, or, for that matter, Anglo-Saxon.

Presently our earlier conversation was resumed. At some remark of mine she smiled. I have never forgotten that smile. It disclosed a front tooth filled with a diamond.

The effect was startling and at the same time evocative. I recalled that the arrangement was affectioned in certain sections of South America, and it occurred to me that the lady might be a Brazilian—a supposition that subsequent developments confirmed. Yet that which at the time intrigued me most was her relationship to the young musketeer. I could have sworn that she would never see forty again, and that he was yet to see twenty-nine. It seemed to me that I must have misunderstood Sally. But a look, which, in a pause of our talk, she shot across the table, undeceived me. It was double-barreled and aimed point-blank at the musketeer and the vision. There was hatred in it. Had I not already likened the lady to a bird I should add that there was venom in it, too. Could a look kill, there would have been murder then and there. A moment and it had gone. Her beady eyes shifted to mine.

A filet of reindeer was being served. From beyond came the rich voice of Monsieur de Malakoff. He appeared to be philosophizing on the degree of decomposition that renders game most savorous. Meanwhile, in the constant replenishment of blond wines, conversation and the tone of it heightened. The young musketeer was still talking inaudibly with that vision, but otherwise the table was united. Topics were tossed like balls. Jests flared as pin-wheels do. Wit, or at least a passable imitation of it, became common property, until, in a ripple of laughter created by a suggestion only a trifle more *scabreux* than the last, Sally rose, and from the gaiety of the room we passed into others yet gayer.

It was not for the sake of gaiety that I was then in Paris. On the contrary, I was at work on a history of the young empresses of old Rome. For such labors there is nothing more serviceable than the Bibliothèque Nationale. Hence the sojourn.

The morning succeeding the dinner I went as usual to the library. The documents that I there obtained held certain stupefactions; but my surprise at what I read was exceeded by my surprise at what I saw. At a table beyond was the young musketeer. Fancy a panther in a conservatory! Yet there he sat, fronted by a pile of MSS., and as lost in them as presently I became in the Subura. When I emerged from that Whitechapel of the past, he saw me and smiled in recognition.

A few days later at the Café Anglais, where, because of its proximity to the library, I was in the habit of lunching, we met again, and in meeting, joined tables. For a while conversation drifted impersonally, but presently the *moi* popped out.

"May I, without indiscretion," I asked, "inquire the nature of your distractions at the Bibliothèque?"

"Alchemy," he answered. "But," he added, with a smile in which there was amusement at my manifest surprise, "let me ask what are your distractions there."

"Nothing half so fascinating," I replied. "I am merely a writer."

"In that case," he retorted, "you are an alchemist, too. A wad of paper and an ounce of ink you transform into bank notes. The transmutation of metals is a process only a trifle more elaborate. Others have practiced it successfully, and what has been done may be repeated."

"No doubt," I answered; "but the age of miracles has gone."

"Has it?" he asked, with an air of great innocence. "That, really, I did not know. I fancied that it had come. I believe that could the people who lived in what you call the age of miracles return they would be far more astonished at contemporary wonders than we are at those of the past. *Tenez, monsieur.* Just across the river is the Église de Ste. Chose. Its construction must have cost a lot, yet it was built by a poor devil of a bookseller who emerged from grinding poverty into abnormal wealth—relatively speaking, that is, for in his time even the richest were none too well off. For that matter, they are none too well off now. It is in wealth alone that the world has not progressed. Kings today have to count the pennies. Budgets are out at elbows. France, the most opulent country in Europe, is obliged to consider penuriously the cost of an ironclad. In early times there was nothing of this. The kings that were built at will cities of enchanted dwellings, shimmering avenues and walls so wide that they were race courses. The treasures that Alexander looted provided him with coin to the value of fifteen billion francs, a sum tolerably large, and yet paltry beside the four hundred and twenty-five billion that is estimated to have been the value of the treasure heaped on the pile of Assurbanipal.

"Whence did wealth in such proportions come? Through what wizardry were the fairylands that existed then created? Obviously, there was a secret, and that secret has been lost. At the beginning of the present era the total amount of money in circulation was a hundred times inferior to that which in earlier days a single satrap possessed. Thereafter the world grew steadily poorer. It was not until after the discovery of the Americas that wealth began to look up. But what are the world's riches now in comparison to what they were? There was not only a secret, and a secret that has been lost, but that secret was the transmutation of metals. Its fading memories used to haunt the minds of men. The attempts of Caligula to regain them are historic. They hallucinated the Middle Ages. Geber's theory, that metals are compound bodies made up of mercury and sulphur in different proportions, fascinated every alchemist, even to Roger Bacon, for he, too, had crucibles, alembics and aludels at work. In Paracelsus the effort culminated. He demonstrated that there was an unknown element, a quintessence, which he called the alcahest, and which when recovered would do the trick. That quintessence, Flamel, the bookseller whom I mentioned, found. I was going over one of his manuscripts today. There, monsieur——"

For a moment he fumbled in his pocket. Then he drew out an envelope, which he handed me. On it were signs quite cabalistic and figures equally abstruse. Yet from it there emanated an odor of orris, and I could not but notice that it was addressed to the marquis at a club. It naturally occurred to me that in addition to the distractions that he admitted he probably had others that he concealed. I am not censorious, and in view of the lady with the diamond tooth, I did not blame him in the least.

"There," he resumed, "are the component parts. I jotted them on that envelope," he interrupted himself to explain, "because it was the only bit of paper I had. But that is the formula."

With that he ran on into technical terms, which conveyed no meaning to me, and my attention wandered until arrested by an entirely intelligible mention of flesh and blood.

"Human?" I asked, with pardonable surprise.

"Yes," he answered, "that is best. But nowadays people have such prejudices. Yet there is the alcahest."

He paused, glanced at the envelope, from it to me, and then, with that grace of manner which only Latins have, apologized for the dissertation. "Anything theoretical is so tiresome," he added, in his winning way. "Yet if by chance the subject has the merit of interesting you, I should be glad if you would accompany me to my shop. My home," he continued, "is in the Avenue Marceau, but for this work I have a *maisonnette* in the Rue de la Pompe, which I fitted up expressly. There I could have the pleasure of showing you an experiment or two."

The stupefactions of the Subura claimed me still. I had counted on a long afternoon at the library. I was stupid enough to prefer the society of a dead empress to a living alchemist, and I thanked him. Whereupon, after paying our scores—scores that included strawberries at a franc apiece, which, mind me now, were fully worth it—we got out into the sunshine and absinthe of the street, where, little dreaming in what dramatic circumstances I was to see him again, we parted.

The dead empress detained me in Paris until, ejected by the heat, I ran down to Étretat. There, at the Casino one noon when looking over the *Figaro*, I jumped as though a dog had bitten me. I think anyone else might have done so, too. I had happened on the account—with which all the world has since been familiar—of the arrest of the Marquis de Parabole for murder.

On the esplanade without was the usual throng of people that gathers there during the hour that precedes the *déjeuner* and succeeds the dip. Among them was my old friend, Mrs. Manhattan. Thinking that I might furnish a fillip for her breakfast, I approached her.

I have sometimes thought that horrors appeal to women more than they do to men. I am often in error; I may have been then, yet, as I greeted this lady, it seemed to me that she was reveling in the revelations. It is true that she knew de Parabole, and acquaintance with people lends an admitted charm to anything that you may read about them. The worse it is the better you like it. Mrs. Manhattan was radiant. From the manner in which she spoke it seemed to me that nothing had pleased her more since the day the news reached her of Sally's engagement. I presumed to say as much, but she turned on me quite viciously.

"When a man kills his wife——" she began.

"His wife!" I exclaimed. "The *Figaro* did not say that."

"Bother the *Figaro*! It was his wife he killed. First he took her money, now he takes her life. If a man marries a Hottentot, then, Hottentot though she be, he ought to treat her decently, instead of which, after making her life a curse, he boils her up in a cauldron."

"Nonsense!" I threw in. "Besides, she isn't a Hottentot; she is a Brazilian."

"It is quite the same to me," Mrs. Manhattan, with superb indifference to ethnology, threw back. "He ought to be drawn and quartered. In my presence once he contradicted her flatly."

"Yes, that is just it," I managed to remark. "A woman will act on a man's nerves day in, day out, and if, under constant fire, his nerves once give way and he calls his soul his own, he is nothing more or less than a brute."

"That's right," Mrs. Manhattan, with great irony, retorted; "that's right. Justify him entirely. A man who murders his wife ought to be decorated. I know all that. I have heard it before. But only in France. And since in France you feel as Frenchmen do, I can't see why you don't run up and congratulate him."

Abashed and hushed, I had no recourse but to retreat. When, a few weeks later, I reached Paris, the preliminary examination had been concluded and the trial was announced. At that trial I determined to be present. Others did, too. So many, in fact, that but a fraction got in. But journalism is a sesame. As a member of the press I succeeded where Members of Parliament failed. I not only succeeded in getting in, I succeeded in getting a seat—a stall, rather. In the interrogatory that ensued a drama unrolled.

For setting, there were bare white walls, which a crucifix dominated. Fronting the audience was the tribunal. There, robed in red, the president and the assessors sat. Before them was a display of exhibits. To the left was the jury. In the dock, to the right, was the prisoner. As I seated myself he looked over at me and smiled, very much as he had in the library. He seemed as out of place in the Cour d'Assises as he had in the Bibliothèque Nationale. There he had suggested a panther in a conservatory, here a prince in the galleys; and I could not but marvel at the intricacies of the mystery we call life, which had led him from one to the other.

These meditations a *greffier* interrupted. The indictment was being read. At its conclusion the president turned to the prisoner.

"What have you to say, de Parabole?"

"That you wish my head, monsieur," the marquis answered, as he rose. "I regret to be unwilling to oblige you with it."

The president pursed his lips and surveyed the court. "That is natural," he answered at last. "But for the moment it is beside the issue. Where were you on the night of the 12th of July?"

"That question I have already refused to answer."

The president pursed his lips again. He reminded me of nothing so much as a salamander. His mouth had the same width and his chin the same recession.

"Yes, I am aware of it," he continued. "You left the *juge d'instruction* to infer that you were occupied with some gallant adventure. For the moment we will let that go, too. Meanwhile you may tell me the object of your separate establishment in the Rue de la Pompe."

"Experimental researches."

"That, I am also aware, is your defense. It is not unadroit. It explains the presence there of an arsenal of chemicals. But it does not explain the presence of other things concerning which you shall have an opportunity of enlightening the jury. You have frequently quarrelled with the deceased."

"If," the marquis answered, "you refer to Madame de Parabole, I do not know that she is dead. Nor," he added, with entire courtesy, "do you."

"I at least know that she is not to be found. The prosecution has searched for her everywhere. But the search was not otherwise fruitless. It has been discovered that at the time of your marriage you had nothing but your title. Your wife, previously a widow, was the daughter of a rich Brazilian. Her property you dissipated. That accomplished, you again had nothing but your title. With a view to bartering it anew you devise an elaborate scheme. You give out that you are an alchemist. You fit up a laboratory. You stock it with chemicals. On the evening of July 12th you lure your wife there. She drives up to the door in her carriage, dismisses it, and enters the house. She has never been seen since that moment. But later that evening a passer hears a scream. At midnight another passer notices a reflection of flame. What were you doing at that hour?"

"I have forgotten."

"Very good. I will tell you. You were destroying the remains of your wife whom you had murdered. But you did not destroy them entirely. In a cauldron in that den of yours were discovered, together with bits of bone, some thick, brown ooze in which were traces of caustic soda and caustic potash. Experts will demonstrate that by means of these chemicals a human body can be converted into just such ooze. Do you deny it?"

"On the contrary, it is quite true. Only in this instance it happens that the ooze was the residue of the body of a gorilla which I had obtained from the Jardin d'Acclimatation."

"That defense you advanced before the *juge d'instruction*. Inquiries made of the management show that you did acquire a gorilla. But it was only a part of this plot of yours. It was only that, in case of misadventure, you might have a ready answer. In any event, the gorilla obtained by you did not, I suppose, have a tooth filled with a diamond. A tooth set with a diamond was found in that ooze. A tooth filled with a diamond was the peculiar characteristic of the deceased. Here it is. I invite you to be seated."

"Silence!"

The court-room, suddenly murmurous with indignation, hummed like a wasp's nest. I could see men gesticulating. A woman fainted.

"Silence!" a crier repeated.

The prisoner seemed unmoved. A fat man approached and addressed him. I heard someone say that it was Maître Dupin, his advocate.

The president, who had reminded me of a salamander, looked now like a wolf; but a wolf that has fed. Turning to a *huissier*, he ordered him to call the first witness, and presently the coachman who, on the night of the 12th of July, had driven the marquise to the Rue de la Pompe was testifying to that effect. He was succeeded by other witnesses—by agents and experts, who corroborated the president's arraignment. When they had gone the *avocat général* addressed the jury, summing up the evidence, deducing from it the guilt of the accused, clearly, logically, without oratory or literature.

"Any question of mitigating circumstances," he concluded, "is out of place in a case such as this. Yet if your conscience hesitates, it is your duty to acquit that man. But if you are absolutely convinced that he is an assassin, it is equally your duty to declare him guilty. I have no wish to say that the blood of his victim cries for vengeance. Of vengeance I know nothing. What I demand of you is justice."

"Silence!" the crier repeated.

Again the room was humming like a wasp's nest. But this time it was murmurous with applause. In the subsidence of that applause the fat man stood up. In his hand he held a paper, at which he glanced. Then he bowed, first to the bench, afterward to the jury.

"Gentlemen," he began, "it had been my intention when I reached here this morning to open my address to you with a citation, not from the code, but from a novel. In the 'Affaire Lerouge,' the most famous story of the famous Gaboriau, a man is arrested for murder. Against him are advanced proofs quite as convincing as those that have been brought against Monsieur de Parabole. But the magistrate having asked him where he was during the night of the crime, and he having refused to reply, the magistrate cried: 'Release him; he has no alibi, he is innocent.' Gentlemen, after reminding you of that subtle and, as it was subsequently shown, correct deduction, it had been my intention to demonstrate to you that the essence of crime is the motive, and that here none has been shown. It had also been my intention to display to you my client in his true light, a young seigneur who, through unfortunate speculations at the Bourse, had lost, not merely his wife's fortune, but his own, and who was seeking to recover both through the transmutation of metals. Whether such transmutation be possible, whether or not—as Monsieur de Parabole has confided to me—he was on the point of recovering that solvent which is alleged to have existed, I am not competent to affirm. But on entering here this morning I did feel competent to use the exhibits that are piled on this table, and to show from them that whether or not the pursuits of Monsieur de Parabole were chimerical, at least they were not criminal. Among those exhibits but one object embarrassed me. That object is the diamond tooth. Even with my client's aid and my best endeavors I felt unable to explain its presence by any theory of coincidences that would have been satisfactory, but it had been my intention to leave it to you to decide whether a man should lose his head because someone else had lost a tooth. These demonstrations that I was prepared to set before you I am now dispensed from elaborating. I let them go, vaguely outlined as they are, for, gentlemen, the Marquise de Parabole is dead indeed, only she did not die in the Rue de la Pompe, she did not die on the 12th of July. She died the day before yesterday in Rio de Janeiro!"

"Silence in this court!" It was the president who was commanding quiet now. There was no longer a murmur, there was a tumult, in which the whole vast room had joined.

"Silence!" he commanded again. Then, turning to Maître Dupin, "What evidence," he asked, "have you in support of this statement?"

"A cablegram brought to me a half-hour ago, which I shall have the honor of submitting to you. Dated Rio, it is addressed to Dr. Rosa e Silva, the Brazilian consul here, and it states that Madame de Parabole died there, as I have represented, the day before yesterday, twenty-four hours after landing. I am aware, *monsieur le président*, that it will have to be verified, but meanwhile I ask that the trial be adjourned."

Mopping his fat face, Maître Dupin bowed and sat down. I could have embraced him. I wanted to tell him so. But the *avocat général* was speaking now.

"The obvious good faith and high professional standing of the gentleman for the defense relieve me," he was saying, "from opposing his suggestion. Yet I must admit——"

What he was about to admit no one heeded. The *salle* was again in commotion. Everybody was talking at once. At the moment I could not see the prisoner. Maître Dupin was bending over him, and presently, through the tumult, circulating above and accentuating it, mounted the shrill call of the crier. Then I became conscious that I had assisted at a *coup de théâtre* which, for sheer poignancy, I had never seen equaled on the stage, and, precisely as from a play, I found myself drifting out with the crowd to the street.

It was months later, in the multiple brilliancies of the Malakoff dining-room, that the last act was given. Meanwhile I had gone to New York and returned. It was June again; and again, in defiance of every canon of precedence, I was seated at Sally's left. Across the table was the young musketeer, and across the table, too, was the delicious vision. On the other side of me was Mrs. Manhattan. From beyond, through the gold branches of the lustres, came the rich voice of the duke. He was philosophizing, as a great noble may, on the superiority of white truffles over black. In appreciating the fine discrimination I could not but reflect that his ancestor, the Napoleonic hero, who had won a duchy with a sword, would have appreciated it still more. These reflections Mrs. Manhattan interrupted.

"There is a subject for you. Why not write it up?"

"Monsieur de Malakoff's physiology of taste?" I asked.

"No; Monsieur de Parabole's physiology of marriage. You know, do you not, that he is engaged to——" and Mrs. Manhattan, with a quiver of the eyelids, indicated the delicious vision. "That is what killed the Hottentot.

The poor old thing knew what was going on. A man may betray the woman who loves him, but never can he deceive her."

"Quite so," I answered; "and it was by way of love-token, I suppose, that she extracted that ornament from her mouth and left it where the police could make the worst of it. When I read in the paper that this lady had first planted her tooth and then vanished in order that he might be guillotined for her murder, mentally I took off my hat to the medievalism of her imagination. But though I took off my hat, were I de Parabole I would have taken her life had she not conveniently died in the interim."

"Oh, yes," Mrs. Manhattan returned, with a suggestion of sarcasm, which at the moment escaped me. "You, of course, would have done wonders."

"But I must ask him," I continued, "whether or not he is still in search of the alcahest."

"The what? The alcahest? What is that?"

"A synonym for happiness," I explained. Then after looking at some blond wine that a footman was serving I looked over at the delicious vision.

"And happiness, to my thinking," I added, "consists, if it consists in anything, in the kiss of one girl."

But my views were unnoticed. Sally was rising, and from the brilliancies of the dining-room we passed to other rooms yet more brilliant.

ONCE IS ENOUGH

THROUGH the eager glitter of Fifth Avenue, Grace Waldron drove to her home. The landau, the liveries, the cherry-bays caught the eye, deflecting it to her. In the transverse stream of traps and motors, women smiled and nodded. On the sidewalk, men turned and stared.

Born a Varick, which is something; the wife of Christopher Waldron, which is something more; currently quoted "among those present"; young, rich, beautiful, intelligent—and, for good measure, not too intelligent—in her radiant landau she represented that which is everywhere phenomenal, an absolutely happy woman. The spiderous Fates who sit and spin are on the watch for such as she.

At the Amsterdams that afternoon, she had had with her Louie May, a young Philadelphian who, since they left Newport, had been stopping at her house. But, during the reception, in the sea of millinery that filled the rooms, the girl had been engulfed. Momentarily she had caught a glimpse of her, stranded at a gold and Sevres heaped buffet and talking there with Nicholas Brevort—an old beau of her own—then, in the rising tides, she had been swept away. Vainly, for awhile, Grace had looked until, concluding that the girl would follow unless she had already preceded her, she had driven off alone.

That evening, Brevort was to dine with them and afterward they were all to go on to the opera, of which it was the opening night. It was yet early, barely five. In spite of the buffet at the Amsterdams, Grace had had nothing and, being healthy, as a beautiful woman must be, she felt she would like some tea, and rather hoped that on reaching home her husband would be in to have it with her.

Her marriage had been a love match. Christopher Waldron enjoyed the reputation of being the best dressed man in town, a reputation, which while perhaps formidable, is perhaps not much to boast of. But Waldron had other qualities. Behind an appearance politely peremptory, that air of being accustomed to instant obedience, he had a manner rarely seductive; the charm which certain New Yorkers used to have and which has gone with old New York. To Grace Varick, imbued by her people with the gentle traditions of gentler days, that charm was myrrh and cassia. Delightedly she had succumbed to it. Since then on her bed of roses not once had she found the crumpled leaf.

Now, as the radiant landau swung along the glittering street, she thought of what she would put on that evening and wondered what Louie would wear. The evening previous the girl had managed to present an appearance of such slim nakedness, that while, in view of that demon, the Mode, there was nothing you could put your finger on—metaphorically, that is—

otherwise there was place and to spare. But that was the fault of Fashion. Louie was as nice a girl as ever lived. A bit too incandescently pretty perhaps, but that was not her fault either. On the morrow she was to return to Philadelphia. It could not be helped, though Chris had protested. He liked the girl, and what he liked was, well, *hors concours*. Nick Brevort probably also liked her. Yet one never knew. Concerning the girl he had been mum. But he was always that way. Had he been less non committal, then, before the myrrh and cassia came, Grace might have been Mrs. Nick.

But now the landau, swinging into a side street, stopped. An automaton, suddenly alive, sprang from the box, bounded like a chamois up the steps, touched the bell, touched his hat, and Grace was in her home— one less spectacular than the Amsterdams, but almost as spacious and perhaps in better taste.

Abandoning her wraps to a footman, she entered a suite of rooms, at the end of which was a room much smaller than the others, consequently more intimate and in which, for that reason, she occasionally had tea. As though to accentuate its privacy, before the entrance draperies hung.

Lifting a portière, she was about to enter, when, with an intake of the breath, she dropped it and moved back.

It is impossible, she told herself. After the manner of those whom the incredible confronts and to whom it always seems unreal, she found but that. It is impossible, she repeated. To assure herself, she was about to raise the portière again when, intuitively, she desisted. Unbelievable as truth sometimes is, she had seen it. To shut it out, she closed her eyes, but, behind the lids, photographed on encephalic films, there they stood, Chris and Louie, his arms about her, in the attitude of a man to whom a girl has yielded, her mouth raised to his.

There is no mistaking that, and Grace misunderstood it so little that now, the sense of unreality gone, one of her selves—the least known to her, the wholly primitive, the animal that is in us all—was inciting her to tear the curtains aside, to rush in, to upbraid and denounce. But the relapse passed as rapidly as it had come. Another condition succeeded it. She felt sick at her stomach. With an effort she dominated that. Yet the effort, exerted on nerves already overstrung, created still another condition. She wanted to get away and hide.

To get anywhere she had to cross the hall, and there were servants. Conscious of that, galvanised, too, by the instinct of form which enables a woman of the world to conceal any emotion, at once, with head erect, she went out. She ascended the stairs, entered her bedroom, locked the door, and at last, securely alone, the instinct of form fell by, another, one more human, asserted itself, tears came, slowly at first, then torrentially.

It was not anger now that she felt, mere wretchedness, the despair which those only know who suddenly find themselves forsaken. Still she wept. Presently, ceasing to be a mere bag of pain and impulse, she re-became the normal woman.

In the first paroxysm she had thrown herself on her bed. Now, the feminine prompting, she stood up, looked in the mirror. The woman behind the cherry-bays, the beauty at whom men had turned and stared, where was she? Her eyes were bloodshot, the lids swollen, the face lined. That was no way to enter into a campaign, she told herself, for, as she had already decided, a campaign there must be.

She rang for her women. An hour later, bathed, massaged, dressed, she planned it.

But, already on the floor below, a counter plot had been organized. Unknown to Grace, Louie through half-closed eyes had seen her. At the sight, wholly momentary, those half-closed eyes had dilated. The girl tore herself from Waldron, indicated the curtains and beneath her breath, less with her voice than with her lips, threw it at him.

"Grace!"

That was all, but it was enough. Waldron straightened, turned, motioned at Louie to seat herself and took up a paper. But his eyes were on the curtains. A minute, another, yet another and still no movement, no sound, nothing.

He rustled the paper. "Aïda! I have supped on Aïda. Let's have some tea."

In speaking he went to the curtains, parted them. Beyond the rooms stretched ornate and vacant.

He turned to the girl. "You were dreaming."

"Dreaming!" she repeated. She had left her seat. At the moment she hated him as only a girl can hate a man who has got her in a scrape. If this thing became known, socially she was dished. "Dreaming! I saw her!"

"I'll ask," said Waldron. He passed through the curtains. When he came back he nodded.

At the nod, she bridled. "You see I was right."

Waldron looked at her. She was abominably pretty, but she was not worth it.

"We'll have to get to work," he announced.

"To work! At what?"

"At getting you out of this."

"And yourself, too."

"I was thinking of Grace."

"What do you suppose she will do?"

"To you? Nothing. Grace is a gentle woman."

"Well, then?"

But Waldron now was looking at the ceiling, from it he looked at the floor. Presently he approached the girl, and to make sure that no one but she should hear, he whispered.

At once the coral of her mouth contracted. Usually her voice was pitched in sol bémol, the tone of it caressed the ear, stirred the pulse. Now, when he had done and she answered, it grated.

"I won't."

Waldron's eyes narrowed. "I am sorry, but we will have to face the music."

She moved back. "Not to that tune then. Old, fat and, what's worse, a pauper! I never heard anything so ridiculous. What would my people say?"

"Damn your people," thought Waldron. But he did not tell her that. Instead, he parried.

"But, when it is all over, they will have nothing to say. Meanwhile you have yourself to consider—yourself and Grace. I said she would do nothing, nor will she, to you at least, except perhaps to cut you. That would be awkward."

At the thrust, Louie, who had been standing, sat down, crossed her legs, tormented the tip of her delicate nose. It would be awkward, very. Perhaps the other way were best. For a moment she considered it, then, with youth's mobility, agreed.

"Very good; though, if between us we muff it, why then——"

Waldron caught her up. "We must not muff it. Fortunately, my part is the hardest, you have but to follow the lead. Before dinner I will send you a box of roses. If, in the box, there is a card, then go ahead, tell her at once."

At the program and the possibilities it evoked, Louie laughed.

"I say, Chris, not roses, lilies-of-the valley. They are more appropriate, more in the rôle, more *jeune fille*."

But Waldron, sure now at least of her, was going. Five minutes later, in a Fifth Avenue club, he was talking at the hall porter.

"Have the operator telephone at once to Florley's for a box of lilies-of-the-valley. Where is Mr. Brevort?"

"Yes, sir. Mr. Brevort is in there, sir."

Squarely in a chair, Brevort sat, as, at this hour, he always sat, looking out on the avenue. He was getting on, moreover; that chair perhaps had made him stout, though less so than a man who was then talking very vigorously to him about nothing what ever.

Waldron approached, joined them. Presently the other man, sufficiently unburdened, got up.

Waldron turned. "Nick, you were at the Amsterdams today."

Brevort turned also. "What of it?"

"You are a friend of Grace, aren't you?"

Brevort turned again. It was his answer. Always he had spread openly before her the mantle of his devotion. There had been a time when she might have been his. But the estate of his father had come to him blanketed in mortgages. Instead of being rich, he had found himself relatively poor. Of that he had said nothing. But talking was not his forte, loyalty was.

"Grace needs your help," Waldron resumed.

"Then it's hers," he said simply.

But now a servant approached and addressed Waldron.

"The flowers are at the door, sir."

"Bring them here."

Adjacently other members were seated. They were not the kind that listen, but they might overhear. After the flowers had been brought, Waldron lowered his voice. What he had to say, he said quickly.

When he finished, Brevort turned on him. "What a damned blackguard you are."

Waldron smiled, waved it away, let it pass. "The point is, will you?"

Meditatively Brevort drummed with his fingers. "It is a large order," he said at last.

Again he drummed. "But not a life sentence, eh?"

Sure of him then, Waldron laughed. "And not hard labor either. My dear Nick, a month, less perhaps. Six weeks, at most. By the way, have you one of your cards, with you?"

Brevort fumbled and produced one. It never occurred to him to ask for what it was to be used. It did not occur to Waldron to tell him.

Waldron opened the box, put the card in it, retied the ribbons, scrawled the name and address, rang for a servant and dispatched it.

Brevort stood up. "I must dress."

Waldron also got up. "I too. You won't have something first?"

Brevort, without replying, stalked on. Waldron followed, left him at the door, entered a taxi and in it sailed home.

Grace meanwhile, regally gowned, roped with pearls, sat alone in her room, maturing her plans. Two hours, that were two eternities, had passed since this thing had battened on her. She was bruised, wounded almost to the death, almost but not quite. She had a rôle to perform and perform it she meant to, without a word, a reproach, a single recrimination.

At dinner presently, afterward at the opera, she would appear as always she had appeared, the portrait on foot of a woman without a care. On the morrow Louie's visit terminated, and she would see her off, smile at her, kiss her good-by. The day after she, too, would go, but to Newport, where she could claim residence and where, without uncivil proceedings, they set you free.

Then Chris must marry the girl. Beyond that she could not see.

On a table beside her a clock struck silverly. She looked at it. It was time to go down. Leisurely, with every evidence of at least outward calm, down she went, entered the drawing-room, approached the fire and absently before it held a hand.

But someone else was entering, she turned. Slim, but less naked than the night before, in virginal white, a spray of lilies at the girdle, demure but incandescent, Louie appeared, and Grace smiled at her

For a second, but for a second only, the smile nearly bowled the girl over. At once she was up and at it.

"Grace," she murmured in that sol bémol of hers, "whatever became of you this afternoon? I hurried back here, found Chris, and he was so delighted that he kissed me."

At the barefacedness of it, Grace flushed.

"What are you talking about?"

"Why, I'm engaged. Didn't you know? Didn't Chris tell you?"

But now in the doorway a footman was mumbling, and Brevort marched in.

With the bubbling laugh of a young faun, Louie, who was nearest, gave him her hand. Before he could address her, before even he could address his hostess, Waldron, entering at his heels, touched him on the back.

"I say, Nick, I do congratulate you. When I heard it I gave Louie a jolly good hug. You don't mind, do you?"

"Did she?" Brevort rather cavalierly inquired, for he was looking at Grace who was looking at him. And what a look! Could bewilderment, uncertainty, then relief, then joy, the abrupt conviction that jealousy had blinded her, that it had all been a nightmare in daylight; could you fancy these things simultaneously expressed in one look; that is what hers expressed.

In the sudden emotion, one hand went to her throat, her lip trembled but she smiled. The other hand she stretched to him.

At once, the wonder of it about her, she asked: "Is it true, Nick?"

At which Brevort, bending deeply over that hand that she might not see he lied, and lied for her, gritted his teeth as he answered:

"When have you known me false?"

Beyond, in silent announcement of dinner, the butler appeared.

"Then come," she cried, "and we will drink your health." Gayly she turned to Waldron. "Chris, you take Louie." In speaking she shook her finger. "But mind! Don't kiss her again. Once is enough."

Louie bubbled afresh, and Waldron smiled at her. They knew then that they had not muffed it.

ALMA ADORATA

"*LES voyageurs pour Paris en voitu . . . rr . . . re!*"

The call rang musically through the night. I had forgotten that the train had stopped. Epictetus was with me. I am familiar enough with him, but he always seems to have something new to say. In that he differs from others of my friends. On a train, he is particularly serviceable. He stimulates your imagination, and that spares your eyes. But, at the call, I looked up, and then at the door of a compartment which I was occupying on the Sud-Express, and in which, thus far on the trip, I had, to my satisfaction, been alone.

Now, a man was entering, assisted by two servants. They got him seated directly opposite me, and then, from the corridor, fetched a lot of rugs and bags which they distributed about. Presently, they vanished. I looked at the man. He was a sallow creature, with great, burning, black eyes, and dressed with that absence of smartness that is sometimes the result of philosophy, but more often of indifference, the which, after all, is a form of philosophy itself. As I was inventorying him, I saw that he was inventorying me. As our eyes met, he smiled. Meanwhile, the train had started.

"You do not remember me," he said, in English. "Yet, of course, I have changed a lot, and you haven't a bit. I am George Capel."

"Certainly, I remember you," I replied; and so I did when he told me who he was. We had been at school together at St. Paul's. That is fully a generation ago. Since then, I had lost sight of him. But, as memory raised a latch, and he emerged from behind it, a scatter of reminiscences trooped after him.

I recalled that his people were disgustingly rich, and that, after Harvard, he had been billeted as attaché to our minister—we had ministers then—at St. James's. In that effulgence he departed. I saw him going in to dinner directly after royals, and discussing with them the disadvantages of not being born. What is worse, I saw him purchasing as many trousers as he liked without fear of interference at our docks. I saw the magnificence of this splendor, and nothing more, for, almost immediately, a change in the White House had been followed by a change in our representatives abroad, and, of Capel, I heard nothing further. And now, there he sat before me. Such are the surprises of life and of *trains-de-luxe*.

"No," he continued, "you have not turned a hair. But, then, what a delightful existence you lead! *C'est beau la vie littéraire.* Whereas I——"

He paused, looked out of the window, then back at me, and asked, abruptly, "You know what happened, do you not?"

"After your recall from London?"

He nodded.

I shook my head. It was quite one to me. But Epictetus admonishes us to be considerate. I saw that he wished to talk, to abuse somebody or something, to use me, perhaps, as a sewer, and I proceeded to let him.

Presently, from the odds and ends of his speech, an idea glimmered. By way of overture, he was executing a fantasy on St. Paul's.

"You remember Manners, do you not? He was in the sixth form when we were in the fifth."

"Yes," I answered, "I do remember Manners, and I remember, too, that he had precious few of them."

"Candidly, he was a brute. That, though, is a detail. After leaving London, I met his sister. How did you feel when you first read Victor Hugo?"

"Sunstruck."

"Precisely. That is the way I felt when I first saw her. In London, I had seen beauty by the acre. But not beauty such as hers. The charm of it was so heady that I reeled. I cried, '*Gloria!*' and my heart answered, '*In Excelsis!*'"

He stopped again, and again looked out into the night. I ventured to prod him.

"Well?"

"Well," he answered, at last, but remotely, as though returning from some inordinate distance; "well, I had cut Manners long before. There was one difficulty, for their parents were dead, and she lived with him. How I bridged that is immaterial. But I did bridge it. Then, I encountered another difficulty. She was engaged. Meanwhile, she treated me as though I were part of the landscape. There was about as much chance of my getting her as of becoming Emperor of the French. Do you mind if I smoke?"

"Not in the least."

"*Eh bien! alors voilà la situation*," Capel continued, when he had found and lighted a cigar. "But there are miracles. By the way, do you believe in ghosts?"

"Everything is possible," I replied. Yet, as I handed out that platitude, I minded me of a lady who, being asked the same question, had answered, "No, but I am dreadfully afraid of them." I am quite as much afraid of bores. I did not say so to Capel, however. Frequentation with Epictetus makes one very civil.

"Yes," Capel retorted, "yes, everything is possible. You are right—perhaps even more so than you fancy; perhaps more than anyone could fancy. For, ultimately, through circumstances which would take me too long to disentangle, there occurred nothing less than a procession of miracles. In the first place, she consented to permit me to vacate the landscape of which I had been a part. There was miracle number one. Then she broke her engagement. There was the second miracle. Finally, she put her hand in mine."

At this climax, Capel, in a crescendo of triumph, stared at me through his great, black, burning eyes.

"Ah," he ran on at once, "ah, the sheer intoxication of the bewilderment of it! The past became a mirror, mirroring nothing save the dream of the coming of her. The future grew wholly solid, brutally beautiful, dreamless and real. While, as for the present, there, fairer than the desire of a fallen god, she stood, her hand in mine."

In the excitement of the retrospect, Capel, with magnificent unconcern, flipped the ashes from his cigar partly over himself, partly over me. But, at once, noticing his carelessness, he apologized and asked would I do him the favor to call his man.

I looked out in the corridor. The servants were seated there with the porter. I beckoned to one of them.

"*A boire*, Ferdinand," said Capel, when the man appeared.

"*Monsieur désire-t-il à manger aussi? Il y a des cailles en aspic.*"

"Will you eat anything?" Capel asked of me, and, on my thanking him, ordered some mandarin liqueur, which Ferdinand presently produced in a flask of gold, and, arranging the little table, with which these compartments are supplied, set it there between us, and with it two little cups, also of gold, which from the workmanship I judged were Deccan.

At Capel's invitation, I took a taste of the liqueur. For a wonder, it was not the imitation. Capel tossed off, one after the other, two of the little cups, and began with his tale anew.

Yet something, the story, perhaps the country through which we were passing, or both, evoked an episode that had aromatized my youth, and, losing myself in it, I ceased to listen.

When, at last, I caught up with him again, I found he had been telling me of the wedding. From what I gathered, it had occurred out of town—at Lenox, perhaps—and, immediately after, he and his bride had driven to the station. On the way, they were run into. Whether by an auto or a trolley I did not hear. In any event, there was a crash. It was the crash that aroused me.

"When I recovered consciousness," Capel was saying, "they were carrying Alma away. She was dead."

"What!"

"Dead," he repeated; and, as he uttered that monosyllable, in which all of life is resumed, he looked down, and in those great, burning, black eyes of his I divined that there were tears.

For a while he sat, his head still bowed. The porter entered, offering to make the beds. I waved him away. But, at the interruption, Capel looked up at me again.

"You will, perhaps, understand what it meant. At the moment she was mine I had lost her. For a shock such as that there is nothing earthly that can palliate or console. My whole life had gone down with hers."

"I do understand," I answered. "Many another would have followed her."

"And do you know why I did not? But how could you know! That which kept me from killing myself was the fact that I did not believe it."

"Believe what?"

"Why, that I had lost her! After efforts on my part, of which the recital is needless, but of which many were hopeless and all inconceivable, there, just when I had got her, suddenly, in an instant, without warning or premonition of any kind, from the carriage in which we sat, from my side, from my arms, she was tossed into death. It was too abrupt. I could not believe it. I told myself that it was not true, that it was a nightmare from which I should awake."

"Yes, yes," I threw in, "I can understand that also."

"When I was able, I got to town, to the house which we were to have occupied. There I immured myself. The servants were told never to approach me. Such orders as I had to give I put in writing and threw out in the halls. Months passed, during which I neither saw nor spoke to anyone. The nightmare was about me still. I was waiting to awake. Everything is possible, you said. Awake, at last, I did."

"Yes, yes," I repeated, "I can understand that, too. For sorrow there is but one cure—time and silence. And," I added to myself, "someone to beguile them both."

But the little *à part* might have been uttered aloud. Capel was too feverishly intent to heed. He was looking now less at me than through me, on some vista visible only to himself.

"I awoke," he continued, "to find that it was not true. You must have read De Vigny," he interrupted himself to remark, "and you will probably recall a passage in which he speaks of a vault opening in the far blue sky and showing a shaft that ran up through millennia, through aeons, and up that shaft he mounted, mounted, mounted ever further yet."

I did not remember the passage, but my interest, that had waned, increased, and I nodded as though I had.

"One night, I, too, mounted that shaft. How? Clairvoyantly, like De Vigny, I suppose. But I cannot be sure. I only know that mount it I did, and that there, very near the summit, among cascades of light, cavalcades of beauty, cataracts of harmony and convulsions of splendor, Alma stood, her arms outstretched. As I reached her, she leaned forward, and down the shaft of azure we sank together, down through lambiencies of amber and emerald, deeper and ever deeper yet, through resplendent perspectives, through pulsations of life unto life, deeper, deeper still, through ascensions of immaculate joy, through tempests of forms and farewells, deeper, still deeper, through diminishing consonances, through the undulations of tumults, the trepidations of passion, through swooning splendors, through interrupted delights, deeper, deeper still, through measureless abysses, through millennia, through aeons, through kalpas of time and of space, deeper, always deeper, further and further yet, until peace slept upon us as dawn upon the sea."

"*Il devient lyrique*," I mused.

"On the morrow, when I opened my eyes, it was to the accompaniment of music. I was in my room in town, and at the other end of it, at a piano, Alma sat. She was playing an air that I had never heard. It was the melody of it that had aroused me. I went toward her. As I did so, I could see that she was fairer than ever, etherealized, aerial, quasi-transparent, wholly divine. As I approached, she turned. The rhyme of her lips parted ineffably, and she smiled. I took her hand, or, rather, tried to take her hand, but my fingers closed on nothingness. At this, she smiled again. In words not articulated, which, however, through some process similar to that of clairaudience, seemed to vibrate within me. 'You forget, do you not,' I heard her say, 'that I am but a spirit now? Yet kiss me. It shall be the seal of our marriage eternal.' At that, she rose to me, and on my lips I felt the volatile caress of a perfume."

Capel had been looking at me, intently. But now his expression changed to one of inquiry. "There is nothing improbable to you in this, is there?" he asked.

I was about to answer that there was, but Epictetus, whom I still held in my hand, restrained me.

"No," I answered, "I see in it nothing improbable. A crustacean extracts from the water substances wherewith to make a shell. From food a bird produces feathers. Similarly, an animal creates bone. These processes are marvelous, yet so common that we give them no heed. But, in view of them, it is quite conceivable that a spirit may so utilize particles and elements of air that materialization ensues. What you tell me is not, therefore, improbable, and as Alma—I beg your pardon—as Mrs. Capel was your wife, there is nothing improper in it, either.

"On the contrary," I added, after a moment, "quite the reverse. But tell me, have you suffered from cataract?"

Capel stared at me, blankly.

"At Heidelberg," I continued, "I remember that my shoemaker became annoyed by the apparitions of deceased, and possibly defaulting, customers. One day, when I was trying on a pair of those magnificent boots that harmonize so beautifully with student caps, he was good enough to take me into his confidence. Had he been an Italian, I should have counseled exorcism; as he was a Teuton, I recommended an ophthalmic surgeon. The surgeon, I subsequently learned, came, examined and operated. In no time, those ghosts were laid."

The stare from Capel's face had gone. He was looking at me now with diligent disdain.

"But your experience," I resumed, "is, of course, entirely different. It accords very perfectly with many another set forth at length by the Society for Psychical Research. Moreover, it is directly in line with experiments conducted by Sir William Crookes. *Ce monsieur n'est pas le premier venu.* He is a scientist. As such, he was, a few years ago, honored by the visit of a young and very pretty spirit, named Katie King. She sat in his lap, decorated his buttonhole with a rose, and told him all manner of delightful things. Said Sir William, in a subsequent monograph concerning her, 'I do not say that such things may be; I say that such things are.' Personally, had I been similarly honored, I should have refrained from publishing anything calculated to reflect on Miss King's conceptions of the convenances. But, then, I am not a scientist. Then, too, it may be that Miss King gave him permission. There are women who like publicity. It may be that there are spirits with similar tastes.

"But apropos," I added, "permit me to ask you a question. We have agreed, have we not, that everything is possible? Let us also agree that everything is explicable. There is no such thing as mystery. There is only ignorance. Now, what I would like to ask is this: may it not be that some of your friends, alarmed by your claustration, and seeking, perhaps, to divert you, succeeded in introducing into your house some—some fairy, let us say, who was fortunate enough to possess a resemblance to your wife?"

From Capel's face, the high disdain had gone. In its place had come that rapt look which mediums share with the insane. Whether or not he had heard my query, I could not tell.

"When Alma kissed me," he resumed, "the music continued, the melody, too, of her inaudible words. It was all quite real—as real, that is, as the intangible can be. There she was; I was kneeling to her, gazing up in her eyes, watching the changing rhymes of her mouth, dazzled by her beauty, transported by her presence, idolizing her with an idolatry no mortal heart has known before, yet unable to touch her, unable to get more than the savor of her perfume on my lips. Real, did I say it was? It was insensate."

"No," I objected, "not that. You had all the raptures of love, with none of the disillusions of life—*l'ivresse du baiser sans le contact des lévres*. And that, believe me, is the ideal. But, if I may ask without indiscretion, did the materialization prolong, or was it renewed?"

"Every day she came to me, sometimes every hour. With colored vapor she reproduced herself, reproduced the gown, the lace, the pearls, the flowers which at high noon she had worn that day in church. Were it not that instead of the silk of her mouth my lips met nothingness—at most but the subtlety of an impalpable perfume—the illusion of her presence would have been complete. At a little distance, her translucence was barely apparent. Though but a vision, she was a distinct delight—to my eyes, at least; to my heart as well. But, otherwise, the fable of Tantalus was accentuated, augmented and multiplied a thousandfold. To behold her near me was beatific, but to be unable to hold her to me was torture sublimated and distilled. It was torture so lancinante that one night I sprang at a pistol, thinking that in death, thinking were my flesh thrown aside like a garment, I could mingle my spirit with hers. Instantly, she was at my side, compelling me to desist, warning me that I was separating myself from her, not forever—no, not that—but until I returned in the Ship of the Million Million of Years."

"What is that?" I asked. "I have never heard of it."

"Nor had I. Nor did she explain. She was not permitted to, she told me later. But the threat of it sufficed."

"*Et puis?*"

Capel waved his hands. "That has been my life since then. She is always with me, when I am alone, that is, and, save an occasional journey taken, as this is, at her wish, alone I always am."

The train was stopping. Through the door of the compartment the porter peered.

"*Bayonne! Dix minutes d' arrêt.*"

Capel started. Yet, that was natural. From the uplands of the occult to a southern prefecture, the distance is appreciable. He had been far away; I, too, and to change the air I got up and went out to the station beyond.

There it occurred to me to enter the buffet and order a *mazagran*. As I passed into the restaurant, a cry followed me, succeeded immediately by the noise of hurrying feet. Turning, I saw a gathering crowd of guards, officials, passengers. I got among them. Capel appeared to have fallen. His servants were lifting him back into the car.

"It is a syncope," said Ferdinand, in French, when we had him stretched out in the compartment, "one of the attacks to which he is subject. Jules," he added, to his comrade, "telegraph to madame to meet us."

"Jules had better stay here," I said. "I will attend to the message. To whom is it to go?"

"To his wife, monsieur; to Madame Capel, 11 *bis*, avenue Kléber. Monsieur is very kind."

"To his wife!" I exclaimed. I felt as though I were having a syncope myself. "I thought—I thought——" Truly, I did not quite know what I did think. "He is recently married, then, is he not?" I managed to ask.

"But no, monsieur. Monsieur and Madame Capel have a son who is going on his eighteenth year."

Thereat, at once, in reply to my heightening and manifest bewilderment, Ferdinand answered me in a manner eminently discreet:

"My master has perhaps been divagating to monsieur. A year ago, he was injured in the explosion of a launch. He hurt his spine, and"—as the man spoke he touched his forehead—"it upset him here. Apart from that, he is good as bread. *Et d'une douceur! C'est un enfant.*"

"*Ah! voilà. J'y suis.*"

I looked down at Alma's adorer. He seemed to be recovering—to be returning rather to that world invisible and fantastic in which poets and mad men dwell.

Such are the stupidities and vulgarities with which the rest of us are surrounded that I envied him the unreal that was real to him. "Cheat yourself and dream," said Epictetus. Capel had known how better than I who have frequented that sage. He had known how better, perhaps, than Epictetus himself. There was indeed reason to envy him, a thousand reasons to envy his immaculate and imaginary amours.

And, reflecting that of all traveling companions—Epictetus included—lunatics are the most stimulating, I went back to the station, despatched the message, and got aboard again, as the guard called through the night:

Les voyageurs pour Paris en voitu . . . rr . . . re!

THE NAMELESS SHAME

"IT is most unusual!" said the Duchess of Kincardine. "Most!" she added. Then, rallying, she exclaimed: "What is the world coming to?"

There had been a stupid discussion that had arisen, how, the Lord only knows, apropos of the tea things, perhaps, on the subject of poached eggs. I had ventured to state that it was sinful to poach them in water, that no one with any sense of self-respect would touch an egg that had not been cooked in milk and mushrooms.

"Why not in champagne and pine-apples?" Agatha, the duchess' daughter, had suggested. "Yes, why not?"

But here solemnities were interrupted. Yorke—the Honorable Eric—a beautifully preserved young man of forty, glided in. "Ferrol is dead," he soothingly announced. "Howdy do? He was found on the floor. Good-afternoon. Thanks, very much. No sugar."

"Dead!" cried a fat, rancid-faced woman, known as Lady Massingbird. "How shocking! And his engagement to Miss Rivers off only yesterday! But what was it? A fit?"

"No," Yorke replied, in the same soothing way. "No. It appears that somebody strangled him."

It was at this juncture that the Duchess of Kincardine made her notable exclamation.

The duchess, it is hardly more than worthwhile to relate, was *née*, as you may remember, not merely *retroussé*, but Genevieve Bridgewater, of Washington Square. The story of her marriage to a Scotch bankrupt is common property. It is also ancient history. So ancient that long since she found time to develop the Kincardine burr, and there-with a perfection of dowdiness which even in London was considered successful. Yet these laurels must have been insufficient. Whether because of her nose, or the immaculate atmosphere of lower Fifth Avenue, in which she had been brought up, or both, or some-thing else, natural ambition, perhaps, she had also succeeded in being talked about. But that, too, is ancient history.

I had known her when she was a little thing in short skirts, and I remember still the spindle legs which she then exhibited. That rather intimate reminiscence constituted my passport to her very dingy house in Hill Street, where, of a June afternoon, she was inquiring what the world was coming to. In London, anything that has not occurred every day since the memory of man runs not to the contrary is always unusual, unless it happens to be most so. The remark of the duchess was, therefore, in accordance with precedent. But in this instance it was justified.

The death of Ferrol—Lord Henry Grafton Ferrol—was, when you got at the facts, not merely unusual and most unusual, but altogether extraordinary. It was the curious circumstance that his engagement should have been broken one day and he should have been killed the next which astounded the duchess and, for that matter, the rest of us who were with her. But that circumstance, however astounding, was tame beside the surprises which followed.

With Ferrol I had had a slight acquaintance, one which had begun in Hill Street and had continued—of all places in the world—in the British Museum. Incidentally, I was also acquainted with Miss Rivers. Like the duchess, she, too, was a New Yorker, a millionairess to boot, and a tip-top sample of what our commerce in beauty can exhibit. Joined to her looks and her dollars she had an air of dauntlessness which, to me, was very fetching, but which, in London, I had heard catalogued as "so American," a phrase which, being interpreted, means, I believe, very vulgar.

Of the breaking of her engagement to Lord Ferrol, I was aware, but not of the reason. On that subject, no one in Hill Street could, I found, enlighten me. It was known merely that the day previous the girl had gone to Paris. But with conjectures I was presently, supplied.

Into the room there had erupted a compatriot, Lady Silverstairs, a delightful little woman, who knew pretty much all that was going and a good deal that was not . . . She too; had heard of Ferrol's death and also of the broken engagement. Concerning the latter, Lady Massingbird was at the moment holding forth.

"It must be, don't you, think?" she indulgently put in, "that either she found out something awful about him or else that he found out something still more awful about her?"

"May not the discoveries have been mutual?" Lady Silverstairs suggested.

"Yes," said the duchess; "but, then, you see even that does not explain how he got strangled."

The word seemed to stir my delightful compatriot voluptuously. "Strangled?" she repeated. "I thought it was rupture of a—of a thingumagig."

"Oh, no," Yorke consolingly corrected. "Howdy do? No. Ferrol's man ran out and saw Simpson in a hansom. Simpson, you know, is the chap who looks after—what? Yes, physician in ordinary. Well, from what I heard this afternoon at the Bachelors' Simpson said that it was due to compression of the carotid artery."

"Where is that?" asked the Lady Agatha, who, with affected precipitance, added, "Don't tell me, though, if—if——"

"Oh, no," Yorke reassuringly answered, fumbling as he spoke at his neck, "it is here."

"But who did it? They don't suspect Miss Rivers, do they? Or did he do it himself?"

'No one knows who did it. But, of course he did not do it: Simpson, don't you see, says that that isn't possible. I dare say——"

Yorke proceeded to lose himself in amiable hypotheses. But presently whipped in by the duchess, he got back again to what he had heard. What he had heard was to this effect:

Ferrol, the evening previous, on returning to chambers which he occupied at the corner of Piccadilly and St. James Street, had dismissed his man for the night. This servant, who had been with him forever, had then gone to his quarters below stairs, and had remained there until the next mornings when, in fetching up Ferrol's breakfast, he found him flat on the floor, the mouth and eyes wide open. Then Simpson had been called in and he, deciding that it was a case for the police, had notified Scotland Yard. The latter had been stumped at once. In the dead man's chambers nothing relative to the crime or to the presence of a criminal had been found, though, from the housekeeper, a hint had been pulled. This woman, the night previous, had been to a music hall. She had returned about one o'clock. In proceeding to her room, which was at the top of the house, she had, in passing Ferrol's door, noticed that it was open. Then, on reaching the floor above she had heard a lady going down. She had not seen her. She had but heard the rustle of her skirt.

Yes, but whose skirt? Murder is painful, but a skirt is demulcent. Whose skirt was it? The question, ping-ponged over the tea things, finally lost itself among them. No one knew anything about Ferrol's clandestine affairs; but then, of a man's surreptitious amours, no one does know anything unless they get in the papers, where they are so generally befuddled that the culprit himself would not recognize them.

Then, too, it may be that Ferrol was hardly the kind of chap to go in for the illicit. To me he had represented a reunion of attributes which I have never found out of England; and not often there—that of smartness and scholarship combined. He knew the world, possibly the devil, but certainly the literature of India which, he read, not in the Clarendon Press translations, but in the original. His scholarship did not stop there. He had produced a work which had gained for him the respect of European Orientalists. It was a commentary on the Soûtras of Patandgali.

138

To a man of that caliber the clandestine and the surreptitious are usually vulgar, and always inane. Yet, then, in the hearts of the best what abysses there may be! There are men, as there are women, dwelling on the uplands of life, who, in spite of the contrast, perhaps because of the contrast, are seized by absolute nostalgias for mud.

Even so, concerning that skirt I had my doubts. Besides, it was yet to be shown that it had rustled from Ferrol's rooms. Of one thing of course, I was certain. It did not belong to Miss Rivers.

That certainty, however, was not shared by Lady Massingbird. On the contrary. It was a visible enjoyment to her to assume that it could belong to no one else. But with these views only Lady Silverstairs agreed.

"There is no doubt of it," declared that delightful little woman. "It must have been hers, unless, indeed"— and here she smiled, and; smiling, disclosed a glimpse of teeth as pretty and as keen as a kitten's—"unless she happened to be flaunting it in a *can-can* at the Moulin Rouge. That would be so like her. Yes, wouldn't it?"

In the ripple of laughter that ensued I got up to go. It did not seem that anything further could be added. Nor was there for a while. At the inquest nothing not already known was developed except that Simpson was an ass, and one equally meagre item. This item was produced by Ferrol's servant, who testified that for several days prior to the murder his master had seemed not quite easy: Asked how this condition had manifested itself, the man made the remarkable statement that Lord Ferrol had instructed him to pitch downstairs anyone that he saw trying to get in.

The item, if meagre, was suggestive. Taken in connection with the main episode, it became dramatic. It showed, or seemed to show, that Ferrol was anticipating, if not what actually occurred, at any rate, something sinister. Then, suddenly that something had come, and as suddenly had gone, leaving not a clue behind, leaving not even a trace, leaving no sign of its presence, no indication of a struggle, leaving nothing but a corpse on the floor, the eyes open, the mouth distorted, a human being choked out of life in a jiffy.

Scotland Yard had become very active. So, too, had the press. The latter dripped with the mystery. Everybody was bewitched by it. It had even the merit of interesting an exalted personage. Meanwhile, no suspicion of any kind rested on Miss Rivers, who; on the evening of, the murder, had, with her retinue, descended on Paris at the Hôtel du Rhin. But though no suspicion attached to her, it was felt in Scotland Yard, and more agreeably still in exalted circles, that, because of the unexplained rupture of her engagement, she might, if she chose, possibly provide a clue.

But the matter was very delicate. For here was a young person, the Stars and Stripes wrapped all about her, who had done nothing save cease to be affianced to a man that was subsequently killed. The police could not approach her. Only diplomacy might. And then only diplomacy of a kind which British embassies lack; for where among them is the Metternich who, without violating every canon of decency, could presume to question the girl?

Nevertheless, it was felt that an effort should be made. That feeling, naturally enough, was induced less by a desire for justice in the abstract, than by the hope that the damnable and haunting enigma of the mystery would be explained. In this the exalted personage to whom I have referred was, as I afterwards learned, as keen for a scent as the police.

Of that, at the time, I was ignorant, and so remained until there came a note from the duchess bidding me again to Hill Street, where I learned, not merely what had been going on, but of a triumph of diplomacy that had resulted.

The diplomat who had effected it was, together with a lot of other people, in Hill Street when I got there. He had, it then appeared, been chosen not by reason of any particular astuteness, but simply because he knew Miss Rivers rather well. This diplomat, whom I had met before, and originally in the arms of his nurse, was Lord Nevis, a son of the duchess, and as nice a looking boy as you ever saw.

At the moment he was gorging himself with sandwiches. But, presently, prodded by his mother, the fruits of his mission—already, as I discovered, displayed in high quarters—were produced.

"Well, you know," he at last began, "Miss Rivers said that the reason—er—the reason why she broke with Ferrol was that he was—er—that he was crazy, don't you know. Yes. That's what she told me. She said that he saw things."

"Fancy that!" murmured the endearing Lady Massingbird.

"Well, not things, perhaps," the young lord resumed; "but people; or, rather, a person. Ferrol, you know, had written a book about—about——"

"The Soûtras," I suggested.

"Yes. Quite so. And this book made the people who believed in them rather nasty, or he said it did. Then he got from Benares a letter—where the dickens is that thing gone now?" the diplomat interrupted himself to ask, and, asking, burrowed in several pockets. "Oh, yes, here it is," he added, extracting a bit of paper on which, seemingly, he had jotted hard words. "Yes, Ferrol got a letter from a yogi who signed himself Anagarika, saying that if, within a certain specified time, he did not make public retraction of the lies which he had printed concerning this—er—this system of philosophy I believe it is, if he did not do that he would be visited by the"—here the lad examined his notes again—"he would be visited be the parapoutra."

"The what?" Lady Massingbird exclaimed.

"The parapoutra."

"What is that?"

"Blessed if I know. But that is what would happen if he didn't."

"Do you know what it is?" Lady Silverstairs inquired of me.

I had not an idea. But though I am an ignorant brute, I saw no use in admitting it.

"Yes," I modestly answered. "The parapoutra is the nameless shame."

"What sort of a shame is that?"

"Oh," I replied, "it is hardly a subject for the drawing-room."

"It must be very chaste, then," Lady Silverstairs joyously concluded, while the young lord ran on:

"Yes, that is what was to happen if he didn't retract. Whether he got in a funk over it or not I don't know, but shortly he began to see things. He told Miss Rivers that one night, on entering his library, he saw a man whose back was turned toward him seated at the table. The man was writing. Ferrol said that he could hear the quill squeak on the paper. He went forward to find out who he was, but when he got to him there was nobody."

"What!" we all exclaimed.

"Yes, that is what he told Miss Rivers. He told her that when he got to the table the man broke like a bubble. That was his expression."

"It is most unusual," said the dear duchess, though whether she referred to the incident or to the simile or to both, she omitted to state.

"Ferrol told Miss Rivers," Lord Nevis continued, "that of course he was rather rattled, but that he was absolutely flabbergasted when, on looking down on the paper which was there, he found written the name Anagarika."

"Then he had written it himself," the Lady Agatha indignantly interjected.

"I dare say. But he did not believe it. What he did believe was that it was written by that yogi and that he had seen him there and seen him vanish. When he told that to Miss Rivers and she saw that he was telling it in dead earnest she broke the engagement, and if I had been her I'll be shot if I would not have done the same."

"Is that all?" Mr. Yorke, who had been ambling about, soothingly inquired.

"What more would you have?" Lord Nevis retorted.

"You see," Mr. Yorke answered, in his consoling way, "it doesn't quite explain—now, does it?—how Ferrol came to be strangled."

Lord Nevis helped himself to a liquor. "No, it doesn't. And when I told them at Sandringham about it *he* said that he didn't like the looks of it all."

"It is most unusual!" the duchess repeated. "Most!"

On this occasion I quite agreed with her, and presently in the general conversation which ensued, after telling her so, I got away.

But the mystery accompanied me. It followed me through Berkeley Square, through the lovely quiet of the spacious street. Then, unconsciously, such knowledge as I had once had of the Patandjali Soûtras emerged from some one of memory's ablated cells. I recalled that these Soûtras taught of union with the supersensible, and of the supernatural powers which that union confer. I remembered that among other things they taught how the devout may exteriorize themselves from the body, project themselves through space, materialize partially or wholly, appear and disappear at will.

Tenets such as these are to the Occidental just so much nonsense. But is it not, I reflected, a beneficent Providence that has enabled us to despise whatever we do not understand? Then, too, may it not be that there are possibilities to which we are blind? May it not be that there are forces of which we know nothing, but which subtler intellects have grasped? May it not be that with those forces there are powers of which we know less, but of which acuter minds make use? May it not be as we learned—or should have learned at school— that everything is possible? And granting these forces and powers and the possibilities of them, might it not be that, among the apes and the peacocks in a grove of the sacred temple at Benares, a yogi was now, perhaps, recovering from a catalepsy, self-induced, during which his entity, exteriorized, had crossed the seas, crouched in that room of Ferrol's, waited for him and strangled him there?

If everything be possible, that is possible, also. If not, then there is, I concluded, but one other solution. The threat of the parapoutra, the meaning of which Ferrol necessarily knew, may have so affected him that he imagined the presence of the yogi, really believed that he had seen him, and then, still more affected by the hallucination and affected more greatly yet by the rupture of his engagement, had, in an excess of desperation, throttled himself.

At the inquest Simpson had denied that such a thing was feasible. But it is feasible. It is a form of suicide of which the old galley slaves and a few modern actors know the art. Histrionically, it is utilized to cause the appearance of suffocation which it produces and which is effected by swallowing the tip of the tongue.

It is that, perhaps, which Ferrol had done. Simpson had testified that death was due to heart failure, superinduced by compression of the carotid artery. Even so, the diagnosis would be the same. But where is the physician, in or out of the witness box, who does not like to air a phrase, particularly when there is no one to refute him?

In this instance a layman could have refuted that ass. Heart failure is not induced by compression of the carotid artery. Only narcosis is. Heart failure may of

course occur, but, in that event, it is merely coinciden-
tal. Yet, assuming that in Ferrol's case it had occurred,
what could have caused it? What but fright? What but
the sinister and sudden return of the intangible something which he had once seen break like a bubble before his eyes—what but Anagarika abruptly clutching
and gibbering at his throat?

Such an adventure might, I thought, induce heart
failure in me; and, if in me, why not in Ferrol? The
hypothesis was so spacious that I luxuriated in it. It
was also so picturesque that I at once gave it preference
over the alternate theory of suicide. It was so unusual,
too, that I determined, when I got the chance, to set
it before the duchess and, while I was at it, to suggest
to her that the rustle of the skirt on the stair had come
from the robe of a priest of Siva.

But, when at last the opportunity arrived, the duchess rather took the wind out of my sails by announcing
her son's engagement to Miss Rivers and declining to
discuss the death of Ferrol any more. Fortunately, or,
more exactly, as luck would have it, unfortunately for
me, Lady Silverstairs was less reluctant. Sometime later
I found myself next to her at dinner. During the initial courses I unfolded the beauties of my hypothesis
which, in the interim, I had had the leisure to elaborate
and to which she was good enough to listen. But when
I got into occultism and pictured Anagarika floating
over the seas, filtering into Ferrol's rooms and finishing
him there, she smiled, providing as she did so, glimpses
of teeth perfect enough to make a saint envious, not of
her husband, but, on the contrary, of any *remplaçant*
the poor devil might have.

"Perhaps you don't believe in yogis," I remarked, in answer to that smile.

"I believe that two and two make four," the delightful woman replied. "I believe that if one yogi could do all that, it would not require more than a rabble of them to take British rule by the ear and conduct it out of India. Did that ever occur to you? No. Did it?"

"It occurs to me," I answered, "that argument is agreeable, but futile, with a woman who talks like Solomon and looks like a seraph. But," I added, "if my explanation explains nothing, Ferrol must have killed himself. In which case, whose was the skirt?"

Lady Silverstairs nibbled at a strawberry and shook her pretty head. "Ferrol did not kill himself," she presently announced. "The skirt, I am told, belonged to a woman who was in his rooms that night!'

"A demi-rep?"

"Oh, dear me, no. A woman like the rest of us."

"But," I objected, "surely it is not supposed that a woman of that kind would act like a wildcat? Such things are not done in Mayfair!"

Again there were glimpses of those teeth. But this time my delightful compatriot laughed.

"What isn't done?" she asked. "Or, rather, tell me what is *not* done? Half the peerage is on the way to the divorce court and the other half ought to be."

To this I hastened to agree. "Of course, there are everywhere—breaches of decorum, shall I say? But between bagatelles of that kind, and doing people up, there is a margin, don't you think?"

But here Lady Silverstairs' attention was claimed by a neighbor. When at last she got back at me it was with the same angelic smile.

"From what I hear," she resumed, "I fancy that the woman in the case had expected to be Lady Ferrol. I fancy, too, that she first frightened Miss Rivers into breaking the engagement and then, disappointed in an effort to get Ferrol to renew an anterior pledge, lost her temper—and he his life. That is the idea, though as yet the proofs are not in. But meanwhile—*entre nous n'est ce-pas?*—the lady is under surveillance. Tomorrow, the day after, tonight, it may be, she will be arrested and we will all assist at the trial."

"How disgusting!" I exclaimed.

"Why, disgusting? Don't you care for trials?"

"Oh, it isn't that," I answered. "But all this eliminates my hypotheses, exiles the occult and dismisses the picturesque. It is that which is disgusting. But permit me. You forget, do you not, that Miss Rivers gave as her reason for breaking the engagement that Ferrol saw things and——"

"Precisely," my fair compatriot interrupted. "And so does she. And knows a good one, too, when she is about it. She did not dillydally much, now, did she, about snapping Nevis up?"

"After all," I rejoined, "it is nobody's business but her own why she broke with Ferrol. But if she invented that beautiful story about Anagarika she has an imagination to beat the band. Though, on the other hand," I added, "Ferrol, on receipt of some letter from Benares, may have told her what those chaps out there are able to do, and what he advanced theoretically she may have accepted as fact."

"Oh, as for that, she is great at accepting. It has been one man after the other ever since she got here. But, now that you remind me, that is pretty much the idea that they have at Sandringham."

"Well, then," I replied, "if that is the inside of it I do wish you would tell the duchess. It would seem to her so unusual."

"But I have told her."

"And what did she say?"

"Nothing. She had heard it before and looked upon it as the most natural in the world."

"There is nothing commonplace about her, is there?" I exclaimed.

But immediately there was a move. Our hostess' was rising. As I got from my chair I was conscious of a sense of loss. Under the table Anagarika lay, pitched there by inside information. In lieu of the splendid possibilities he had evoked I had an inkling of a stupid crime. The exchange was not compensatory. I regarded it as a swindle—as worse yet, a nameless shame.

THE SILVERSTAIRS

I

"DR. VANUXEN," Silverstairs was saying, "I should like to consult you regarding a curious case."

Dr. Vanuxen was a little man with the beard of a satyr and a ferret's restless eyes. Silverstairs was not quite six feet and not quite handsome. But he was good to look at, fair and bright.

The room was dim and big. It gave on Mecklenberg Square. In London there are a hundred squares just like it, a thousand rooms just like the one in which these two men sat.

"I have the honor of knowing Lady Silverstairs," said the little man, who spoke with an American accent, "and Lady Silverstairs, I take it, is your wife."

"And a compatriot of yours. It is for that reason I am here. Yes," Silverstairs resumed, "the case is not merely curious, but complicated."

But that you may understand what was behind this case, it should be noted that while all London was open to Silverstairs, there was but one place where he wanted to be, and there he was not wanted. That place was his town house. It was large, commodious and very depressing. In it was his wife.

His marriage to this lady, formerly Hilda Hemingway, of New York, created, as you may remember, an interest not merely local but national and even international. Miss Hemingway was a sort of celebrity. Already she had refused a duke, and also, by proxy, a king. The duke, whose deportment was so deplorable that had he not been a peer you might have mistaken him for one, was so cut up that he swore he would blow his brains out. Of course he did nothing of the kind. The king did not either. His subjects relieved him of that bother.

In refusing these people Miss Hemingway showed, therefore, but ordinary common sense. At the same time, it is not everybody that has the chance. Particularly that of going down into history as a murdered queen. Yet, though the girl missed the rôle of heroine in that splendid drama with which the papers dripped two years ago, providence, or her parents, had provided certain compensations. She was very rich and very pretty. But not beautiful, I have heard women, to whom such attenuations are appeasing, remark.

Miss Hemingway was not beautiful. She was worse. Beautiful women, don't you think, are like overgrown angels, candid, stupid and large? Hilda had the waist of a willis, the face of a fay, eyes that bewildered, and a mouth that bewitched. In spite of which she was so many removes from a coquette that she had not a flirtation to her credit. Men in droves had knocked at her heart in vain.

Yet, when Silverstairs happened along, she accepted him without hesitation, but also without fervor. Silverstairs had lived the life of an English gentleman. He had figured in un-civil proceedings twice. Twice is enough. It was understood that he had had his fling. Moreover, he was an earl. An earl makes a countess. A countess may not wear a train as long by a yard as a duchess, and she lacks, of course, the regalia which queens display. But the position is more comfortable. You have all the fun going and none of the fuss. You are distinctly Somebody without being It.

The position has other advantages. However unducal a duke may be, a duchess is assumed to be too disdainful to heed. Whereas it is not considered bad form for a countess, should she so desire, to get a divorce. Then, also, in the present condition of English society the possibility of murder is remote. All of which had its weight with Hilda, when, after refusing other notables, she accorded Silverstairs her hand.

It was such a delightful little hand, delicate, fragrant and cool, so cool indeed that she seemed unaware of the warmth with which he pressed it. Her face, too, was cool. Wary also. She was afraid of a kiss as of a bee.

This, of course, was not exhilarating. But, then, her appearance soothed. She looked as though she had descended from an elysium created by artists and milliners, some paradise of beautiful confections in which the peris, being blissful to look at, are dispensed from doing anything else. Such an occupation is not fatiguing. Even otherwise, it is the opinion of pundits, that when a girl has succeeded in being pretty she has fulfilled every duty in life. That opinion lovers sometimes share. Husbands, never.

Silverstairs was a lover. In taking him as such, and in taking him, too, without fervor, Hilda had told him that she was not of a fervent nature. But Silverstairs was not alarmed. He had read somewhere that when an American girl loses her heart she keeps her head. Having seen the statement in print, he took it for gospel.

He took ship, too, followed the girl to Fifth Avenue, where the wedding occurred and then piloted her back to London. It was then June. London is not far from the North Pole. But in June you occasionally fancy it nearer the tropics. In the air are the same languors, the same caresses and spells. Such influences are emollient. But they did not affect Lady Silverstairs. On the contrary.

One evening, after a dinner in Catty's menagerie, as the quite hospitable house of the Duchess of Kincardine is called, she and Silverstairs had gone on to the opera.

Hilda was in white. In her hair and about her neck and arms were ribbons of diamonds. Silverstairs could have eaten her. As they entered their box the curtain was rising on the fourth act of the "Hugenots." During the uproar of the claptrap Benediction, Silverstairs twirled his thumbs, but, as the duo which ensues began, he turned to his wife. In the beauty of that enchanting score so potent were the emotions which the cascade of melody evoked, that he stared, wondering were she not also conscious of the vibrations. But the lady was promenading her glass here and there, inventorying the house, distributing little uplifts of the chin to this acquaintance and to that.

Silverstairs was nineteenth of his name. Whether or not Hilda had had a presentable grandfather he was unaware. Yet had she, like the chimerical Clara Vere de Vere, been a daughter of a hundred earls, she could not have looked more absolutely patrician. How the climate of Manhattan can so perfectly produce that which quarterings so infrequently provide, was a mystery to him, as it has been to others. But the mystery of that phenomenon was lost in another. She still kept her head and with it her heart.

The violence of the love which tenor and soprano were parabolating from the stage, may have accentuated this exclusiveness. Anyway, the pulsating harmonies which left her unmoved stirred him.

"Hilda," he began, when, the opera over, they were driving to their residence in Belgrave Square, "Hilda, there is a story of a man who fell in love with a statue. So great was his love that the statue became human, became flesh and blood, and in love with him. Do you see any difference between the statue and yourself?"

"Rather," Hilda answered. "Don't you? The age of miracles is gone."

"Do you mean that you——"

But the brougham had stopped. The door was being opened. Other doors were opening beyond. Hilda passed from the carriage into the house and up a wide stairway that led to the floor above. Into a sitting room which she then entered, and which, for her especial use, had been elaborately refitted, Silverstairs followed. Closing the door, he threw his arms about her. "Tell me——"

Undulantly she freed herself and, moving back a step, looked him in the face.

"Would you mind not mussing me up?"

"Is that your answer?"

"But how odd you are! We went over all that in New York. I told you then that I did not care to be kissed. It is fatiguing to be forced continually to repeat it."

Silverstairs strangled an oath. Earlier earls of his name might have strangled Hilda. Behind the earlier earls was the long line of brutes that stretch behind us all, and who have given us teeth and nails which in them were fangs and claws. At the moment an uprush of the mysterious influences which, for lack of a better term, we call atavism, seized him. The room became flooded with carmine. But instantly the influences retreated, the rich hue faded, the room was quite as before. At once in an effort to display a composure which he lacked, he cast mentally about for some futility, and, hitting on one, inquired, "Who was the man with a beard that I saw coming from here yesterday?"

Hilda first stared, then laughed. "You are not going to be jealous, are you? Oh," she ran on before he could answer, "because I am not in love with you, you need not fancy that I am, or have been, or shall be, in love with anyone else. *Pas si bête!*"

Silverstairs nodded. Outwardly now he was quite composed. Yet, to fortify the composure he returned to the futility anew: "But who is he?"

"An American I met at Catty's, a scientist named Vanuxen. He knows my father. Catty calls him Cagliostro."

"Ah!" said Silverstairs. "Do you mind if I smoke?"

"I think I will go to bed," Hilda answered. "Good night."

Silverstairs opened the door for her. Barely had she gone before atavism claimed him again, vehemently, irresistibly. Slamming the door with a din that had in it the clatter of musketry, he picked up an unoffending little gilt chair and smashed it to bits.

It was the next day, after certain inquiries at Catty's, that he consulted Dr. Vanuxen.

II

"Yes," Silverstairs was saying, "the case is not merely curious, but complicated. With your leave I will put it hypothetically. Supposing a man marries a girl who does not care for him. Is there any way in which he can make her?"

"Make her care for him?"

Silverstairs nodded.

"There are so many that they constitute an embarrassment of choice. But permit me, does the lady care for anyone else?"

"No. There is nothing of that kind. Her attitude is not due either to any fault of his. She is simply indifferent, and told him as much before they were married."

"Why, then, did they marry?"

Silverstairs made a gesture. "Well, you see, he was taken with her and she rather felt, I suppose, that, as a married woman, she would have greater freedom than she could as a girl."

"Yes, here, no doubt. But hardly in the States."

"But," Silverstairs objected, "I did not say that she was an American."

"No," Vanuxen retorted; "no, of course not. Yet then it is only American girls that get these notions. Though, as a rule, their indifference more often succeeds marriage than precedes it. In such cases I have found jealousy highly efficacious."

"What!"

"Yes, jealousy on the part of the lady, complicated by indifference on the part of the man. Indifference is very winning. Men, you know, make the mistake of swearing and stamping about. Tributes of that kind heighten a lady in her own esteem. But when the man is civil, cheerful, smiling and apparently occupied elsewhere, the self-esteem of the lady dwindles to such slight proportions that she could find room and to spare for it on the head of a pin. The cure then is certain, unless—permit me. I assume that the lady gives no reason for her attitude, and that you cannot imagine the cause. Am I correct?"

Again Silverstairs nodded.

"Has she any sisters?" Vanuxen resumed.

"She is an only child. Her mother, by the way, is dead."

"What sort of a woman was her mother?"

"Very charming, I have heard. But I heard, too, that she was rather neglected by this lady's father, and the neglect preyed on her mind. It did not drive her insane exactly, but, if I have the story straight it induced a form of melancholia that resulted in her death."

Vanuxen drew a breath of understanding and plucked at his beard. He seemed to have heard the story before. As a New Yorker the circumstances were perhaps more familiar to him than to the English-man. "I see," he presently remarked, "and, as a girl, this lady was cognizant of the facts, was she not?"

"I suppose so."

"Then you may suppose, too, that they impressed her, and impressed her, moreover, at an age which is the most impressionable of all. To that impression her present attitude is due."

"But I don't see how."

Vanuxen again tormented his beard. "This lady has been a witness to one of love's disasters. She witnessed it in her own home and what occurred there she probably decided must occur everywhere. As a consequence she has argued that, to avoid disaster, she must steer clear of love. In that she is perfectly logical. She enjoys herself, does she not?"

"Very fully, I should say."

"Only you, of course, do not. That is logical, also. We always want what we have not got. Probably if your wife adored you——"

"But," Silverstairs hotly interrupted, "I did not say it was my wife."

"No. But then, you come to me for advice. It would not be worth much, now would it, if I did not appreciate the box you are in?"

"Well, then," said Silverstairs, simply, "can you get me out of it?"

"Are you willing to take a chance? Let me see. Say one in fifty?"

"Of what?"

"Of an accident. But with, mind you, in case there is no accident, the assurance that she will change her views."

Blankly Silverstairs stared. "I don't understand you."

"It would be odd if you did," Vanuxen rejoined. "Yet in a case not similar but cognate I effected a cure. It was the case of a woman who had a very real and a very great grievance against her husband. I was fortunate enough to be able to ablate that grievance as though it had never been."

"Oh!" said Silverstairs, "now I understand. You mean hypnotism."

Condescendingly Vanuxen smiled. "I mean nothing so claptrap and futile."

"Then what the deuce do you mean?"

"Only what I say. If you are willing to take a risk that is possible, but not probable, I can guarantee that in the absence of an accident the attitude of Lady Silverstairs will be the reverse of what it is. If it is not I will not charge a ha'penny."

"But otherwise?"

"It will be £10,000."

Silverstairs looked down and away.

"The sum may seem——" Vanuxen with an apologetic shrug was about to resume, but Silverstairs looked quickly up.

"Oh, bother that. I was thinking of the risk."

"That's right," said Vanuxen, encouragingly. "Think it over. I can call on your wife at any time."

III

"Happiness consists in being on good terms with yourself."

Dr. Vanuxen two days later was enjoying a cup of tea in Belgrave Square, and, incidentally, a chat with Hilda.

"There," he continued, "is a definition which you will not find in the dictionary."

"Ah, yes," Hilda negligently replied. "It has always seemed to me that the people who make dictionaries have at their disposal so much space and so little imagination."

"So little sense, too. Happiness is the world's desire. But though they tell you how to spell the word, never do they tell you how to find it."

"They are frightfully ignorant."

"And equally stupid. It would be so easy to indicate love as the essential factor."

"Of being on good terms with yourself?"

"Assuredly, and of being on good terms with others."

Hilda laughed.

"You do not agree with me," Vanuxen resumed. "Yet, after all, why should you? Besides, when people do agree with me I feel that I am in error."

"You are so indulgent," Hilda threw in.

"And you, Lady Silverstairs, are so skeptical. But skepticism is one of the charms of youth. When you are as old as I am you will believe in any number of delightful things, particularly, perhaps, that in affairs of the heart we are none of us free agents."

Hilda laughed again. "Anyway, I am not quite up to that yet."

"Of course not. Moreover, I am not wicked enough to bore you with demonstrations. But a theory that used to be held may have the merit of entertaining you. It is to the effect that in the high heavens we each have a star whose rays form an enchanted circle in which our loves unfold."

"How spacious and dreamlike!"

"We may do what we will," Vanuxen continued, putting down as he spoke the cup that had inspired these remarks, "we may do what we will to resist the mysterious magnetism of these rays. It may even be that we think we succeed. But, whatever highways or byways we tread, at the end of the journey it is always the one whom our star has chosen that we find there waiting for us."

Carelessly Hilda patted a yawn, and then as carelessly smiled.

"No dodging permitted, I suppose. But my levity is shocking. Forgive it. The theory seems eminently conservative, yet I can hardly fancy that anyone takes it very seriously."

"That is because nowadays no one takes anything very seriously, except the pursuit of happiness, in which we are all engaged, and which, barring those who love, only the gods ever realize."

"And they never lived."

"No, they never did. Oddly enough, though, I was thinking of one of them just before coming here. For I happened on an extract of quinces, an odor which was very fashionable in the very old days and which was called the Perfume of Eros."

"How perfectly poetic!"

"Yes, and for that reason I ventured to bring it, thinking, perhaps, you would do me the honor to accept it. Will you?"

"You are too delightful in addition to being the most extravagant man I know. The Perfume of Eros will be quite a novelty to me."

"Oh, as for that," said Vanuxen, grimly, fumbling, as he spoke, in a pocket, "I am sure of it." From the pocket he produced a little bottle. "Here it is," he added. "But permit me. The odor is more appreciable in a liquid. The tea in your cup is quite cold, is it not? Yes? So much the better. Pour in a few drops, then drink it, and you will taste the fragrance."

With an air of endearing meekness Hilda did as she was bid. She unstoppered the bottle, poured a few drops of the contents into her cup, put the bottle on the table and drank the mixture. Then she made a little face.

"Why! "she exclaimed, "it tastes of ether!"

But, surprising as was the statement, Vanuxen did not seem to heed it. He sank back in his chair. At that moment a diversion occurred. Silverstairs was lounging in.

"Will you have some tea?" Hilda asked. "Dr. Vanuxen," she continued, indicating the bottle, "has brought me a new perfume."

Silverstairs stretched a hand to pick it up. Before his hand could reach it, Vanuxen's had, and then, how it happened the deponent cannot say, but it fell, and falling, broke, musically, after the fashion of little bottles.

162

Instantly Vanuxen whipped a handkerchief out, and pressed it against his nose and mouth.

"But you don't like the odor?" Hilda, perplexed by the mummery, inquired.

Vanuxen sneezed, or pretended to. "Immensely," he replied. "But I seem to have caught cold. I must be going." As he spoke he stood up and bent over Hilda's hand. In a moment he had departed.

IV

"People never die of fever," Vanuxen was saying. "No, they die of physicians, of apothecaries, of idiots. But of fever, never!"

In a room beyond was Hilda. A fortnight had gone since the episode of the bottle. A trifle over a week after that incident she had become abruptly languid, conscious of a malaise, dull at first but slowly accentuating, and, therewith, of a contraction about the temples that generated a form of stupor in which there was dread.

What it was she could not tell. At the time she was dressed for a dance. At dinner she had eaten nothing. In the afternoon there had been an odd creep in the palm of her hands. At table she had felt her face flush. Prior to the dance there were adjustments which her frock required. These her women were arranging, when, abruptly, her brain seemed to tip.

"What is the matter with me?" she asked.

As she spoke she stared at the maids and they at her. Then at once the horrible fright of those in love with life to whom the fear of death appears, possessed her.

"Who is that?" she cried.

Between her and the mirror, before which she stood, a man had surged. He was smiling and offering her his arm.

"Who is that?" she cried again.

The startled servants were staring now at each other. The man, balancing himself on one foot, smiled in her face. She stretched her hands to protect herself from him. But, vaporously as he had come, he evaporated. Night seized her, a night into which delirium stalked.

The delirium lasted for days. It was during an abatement of it that, in an adjoining room, Vanuxen was declaiming to Silverstairs on general imbecility. Among the idiots denounced, Silverstairs obviously was included. But that he was too angry to notice.

"Not for a second would I have dreamed of consenting had you told me that you were to poison her. As it is——"

"Poison! Poison!" Vanuxen threw back, glaring at Silverstairs as fiercely as Silverstairs was glaring at him. "But that is the way with you all. You none of you know the uses of language."

"I say 'poison,' and I repeat it. There was poison in that bottle."

"In what bottle?"

"In the bottle that fell and broke. I saw you clap your hand to your nose, but even then——"

"Poison in that!" Vanuxen shouted. "Poison in my Perfume of Eros! Silverstairs, if we were in any other country in Europe I would have gone out. Poison indeed! Pathogenic bacilli, yes. Pathogenic bacilli all you like. In that bottle there was quite a little family of them. But poison! Frankly, Silverstairs, you are an ignoramus."

"And you, Vanuxen, are a criminal. If my wife dies you shall swing for it."

"I shall swing, then, in poor company. You are an accessory before the fact. When you first came to me I told you there was a chance in fifty. I told you to think it over. You came back and told me to go ahead. In the next room my secretary sat, the door open between."

"I will swing, too, then, if need be, but you shall swing first."

"Meanwhile, what with your confounded stupidity, you have so thoroughly disgusted me that I have a mind to chuck the whole thing."

"And kill her, anyway. No one but yourself knows what the fever is——"

Vanuxen snorted. "That imbecile Saunders whom you had in behind my back first diagnosed it, I think, as typhoid and, afterward, was not, eh, quite so sure."

"Saunders," Silverstairs irrelevantly protested, "is physician-in-ordinary."

"He is an ordinary ass. I won't have him here, or anyone else, if I am to go on. I won't. Do you hear me? And if I do go on, I want you distinctly to understand that it is solely for your wife's sake and not at all for yours. And as for your inane threats and inaner impertinence of your manner, I may tell you now that for the first time I thoroughly understand and as thoroughly appreciate the attitude of Lady Silverstairs."

To the roots of his hair Silverstairs colored. Had Vanuxen struck him he could not have hit him more squarely between the eyes. But, as the phrase is, he was game. He saw that the rebuke, however brutal, he had provoked.

"Were we in the street," he said, "and you," he added, "a bit younger, I would thrash you. But," he continued, "you are in my house. I am sorry to have forgotten it."

V

"How is her ladyship this morning, Harris?" Vanuxen, a month later, was inquiring in Belgrade Square.

"Thank you, sir. Quite the same, sir."

"She will begin, now, soon to pick up," Vanuxen continued, as the servant took his hat and stick. "Is his lordship at home?"

"Yes, sir. Thank you, sir. His lordship will be in the library, sir."

Preceding Vanuxen, Harris showed him into a beautiful room in which there was not a book to be seen.

Silverstairs, who was standing, turned dejectedly as Vanuxen entered.

"Well?" said the latter.

"Oh, it is no use," Silverstairs with moody melancholy replied. "Her mind is a blank."

Cheerfully Vanuxen plucked at his beard. "Did you ever hear of Condillac?"

Silverstairs shrugged his shoulders.

"Condillac," Vanuxen resumed, "was a philosopher. He undertook to analyze the human mind. For the purpose he imagined an adult capable of experiencing every emotion and of appreciating any idea, but having none whatever, and into the mind of this person he proposed to introduce the apperception of things, singly, one after the other. Theoretically, the project was excellent, but practically it was impossible. He had no such person to operate on, and being not a scientist but a philosopher, he was unable to create one. What he could not do I have accomplished. The fever has emptied the mind of Lady Silverstairs of everything that was in it. It is a blank, as you say. But a blank made of wax. Wax to receive and marble to retain."

"Yes, I know," Silverstairs with weary hopelessness replied. "So you have told me, but——"

"But then it was not time to begin. Now it is. Now is the time to put the theory of Condillac into practice. I will show you how. I will show you in the fullest detail. Then, little by little, the education of your wife will proceed. Little by little she will become what you wish. Little by little your ideas will be implanted in her. In her subconsciousness will be the latent memory of things, and from that store you can draw whatever you like, and whatever you do not like you can leave there. You will find, too, the occupation ideal. You will be fashioning a nature in harmony with your own, creating a heart that will be your own heart's image."

Vanuxen stopped, for breath perhaps, and nodded triumphantly. "*Et avec ça?* Is there anything else? Oh, yes, I forgot. Presently you will have the voluptuous and abiding conviction that throughout the civilized world there is not a husband, not one, who, if he knew would not envy you as no husband has been envied before."

Vanuxen stopped anew and nodded again. "But, by the way," he immediately resumed, "have you ever read Rivarol? No more than Condillac, I suppose? I could have sworn it. Said Rivarol: 'Of all women there is only one that is really disagreeable, yet, how odd it is that every man gets her for himself.' From that general law you will be exempt. You will be—but, what is that!"

Through the quiet of the house a cry had been flung, followed now by the sound of voices, the noise of hurrying feet.

Silverstairs rushed to the door, Vanuxen at his heels. In the hall a woman was running. At sight of them she stopped, turned and, running still, led them to another room on the floor of which Hilda lay, her lips half parted, her eyelids closed, waist supported in a nurse's arms.

"She is dead!" cried Silverstairs.

"Her ladyship fell," the nurse explained, "and she has hit her head."

But already Vanuxen was at her side. As he knelt to her those eyelids opened. Hilda looked at him, then at Silverstairs, then at a mirror beyond.

"I thought there was a man there," she murmured. "I thought we were going to Catty's. I thought——"

She hesitated, murmured inaudibly, and her eyes reclosed.

"She is dying!" cried Silverstairs.

But to Vanuxen it was a long time since she had been so thoroughly well. In the shock of the fall it was clear to him that her senses had returned, that her mind was no longer a blank, that the theory of Condillac was useless now, the Perfume of Eros also.

Here was an accident on which he had omitted to count. He got up, walked to a window, looked out at the peace and quiet of the square, and at that tranquillity swore.

Then he wheeled. "Put her to bed," he ordered. "Let her sleep. When she awakes she will be herself."

VI

"Dr. Vanuxen, my lord," Harris announced, "and will your lordship see him?"

"No."

In the library Silverstairs and Hilda were seated. Bewitching always, the illness from which now she had but recently emerged had left her, if possible, yet more enthralling. Since her recovery this practically was the first semblance of a *tête-a-tête* that Silverstairs had had with her. The interruption annoyed him.

"Damned scoundrel," he muttered, as the man withdrew.

"Who?" Hilda asked. "Harris?"

"No; Vanuxen. Though I don't know that I am much better. Do you remember that night we came from the 'Hugenots'?"

On Hilda's lips was the pink of the sea-shell. Into that pink a smile bubbled. She nodded.

"Do you remember what you said?"

Hilda nodded, smiling still.

"The next day I saw Vanuxen. I put the matter before him. He said he could change your views."

"What!" Exclamations and questions shot from Hilda's eyes. Into the sofa on which she was seated she seemed to retreat. Silverstairs, who was standing and who had seen the smile, saw now that it had gone. But he had something to say, and he said it.

"I gave him carte blanche. The result was your illness."

"I don't understand you."

"Nor did I understand him. Not for an instant did I imagine anything of that kind. None the less, I occasioned it, or rather my stupidity did. Or, perhaps more exactly, my hopelessness of you. Yet had you died I would have shot myself. As it is, no doubt you will leave me. I deserve it. Besides, now that you are well again, what happens to me is quite one."

In Hilda's eyes questions and exclamations had multiplied so inordinately that, really, there was not room for another.

"Of course," Silverstairs continued, "you will appreciate that if I have not already given you the facts which, in honor, I owe you, it is because I had to wait until you were sufficiently well to receive them."

Then, at once, summarizing the episodes and incidents which have been already set forth, those facts he recited.

"I suppose," he wound up, "that when Vanuxen called a moment ago it was in regard to his—h'm—to his dishonorarium. I had agreed to give him £10,000. He ought to be glad he is not in stripes. I, too, for that matter."

On Hilda's features waves of emotion had come, broken, retreated and returned. But at this they swept over her. A hand went to her eyes, her slight frame shook and, burying her face in a cushion, she burst into tears.

Into tears, if you please! Silverstairs would have preferred invective. He felt like a beast. Presently, for her consolation, perhaps, too, for his own, he said so.

At that, in the cushion in which she had hid her face Hilda's head shook. She was saying something, what he could not tell, and he bent toward her. One little hand that had held the cushion moved back and out. It seemed to be groping aimlessly, for comfort, perhaps, and tactlessly, as men do such things, he caught it in his own. But, instead of drawing away, the little hand drew him nearer, nearer, yet still nearer, until actually his arms were about her and his lips on hers.

So do miracles occur.

But the marvel of it Hilda interrupted.

"You are a goose," she declared.

"What?"

"Yes. I knew it that night when you slammed the door and broke things. But I never would have known that I was, also, had I not had recently such a lot of time to myself. Such a lot of time to think things over. If only for that I am glad I was ill."

"You are glad!" Silverstairs, in a *crescendo* of bewilderment, repeated.

"Yes, glad. All the while I kept recalling something that had been told me, something about the high heavens where we each have a star whose rays form a circle in which our loves unfold. And we may do what we will to resist them, and it may even be that we think we succeed; but, whatever highways or byways we tread, at the end of the journey it is always the one whom our star has chosen that we find there waiting for us.

"Yes," she added, "all the while I kept recalling that, for I knew our journey was over. Yet, as I realized that, I realized also that I might have died before I had lived, before I had lived to know it."

"Before I, too, had lived to know it," said Silverstairs. But he spoke with quickening pulse. The story flushed him with surprise. He could not quite make it out. He got Hilda to tell it again. Then again. Each repetition flushed him.

"Yes," she announced for the third time, "the journey is over. I know it now. But had I not been ill I doubt I should have known it at all. So you must send Cagliostro his money. It is worth it. Isn't it? Or don't you think so?"

"It is worth all I have. And more, much more. But——"

"But what?"

"There is another journey," Silverstairs continued, gazing at her as he spoke with grave yet insatiate eyes. "One which, if I can help it, shall never be over. It is our honeymoon. Tell me, where shall it take us?"

"Why should it take us anywhere?" Hilda replied. But at once, divining that the query must sound rather subtle, she added, "Belgrade Square is so nice!"

Yet, as Silverstairs seemed to have nothing to say to that, she sniffed and smiled and exclaimed:

"Why, yes! It is full of the Perfume of Eros."

CPSIA information can be obtained
at www.ICGtesting.com
Printed in the USA
BVHW041745170622
640073BV00008B/336